ELLA
on the OUTSIDE

CATH HOWE

ELLA
on the OUTSIDE

nosy
crow

First published 2018 by Nosy Crow Ltd
The Crow's Nest, 14 Baden Place
Crosby Row, London SE1 1YW
www.nosycrow.com

ISBN: 978 1 78800 033 8

A CIP catalogue record for this book is available from the
British Library.

Printed and bound in Great Britain by Clays Ltd, Elcograf S.p.A
Typeset by Tiger Media.

Papers used by Nosy Crow are made from wood grown in
sustainable forests.

To all the children who have
ever felt 'on the outside'
C. H.

Chapter 1
New Girl

Dear Dad,

When I look up into the sky some days, I feel better because I know it must be the same view for you when you look up. If you saw a bird, maybe it would be flying over my house a bit later on.

But then, other days, it's worse. The sky seems so big it makes me feel as if you are a very, very long way away.

Do you think we could both always look out at the sky at the same time each day, like, maybe, seven o'clock in the morning? I think that might help. Shall we choose a time? Shall we do that, Dad?

Love, Ella

"Hellooo, puss."

I stepped across the grass towards the grey cat under the tree and held out my phone to get a picture. I clicked my tongue.

She turned her head. Perfect! The sunlight was falling on her back just right, lighting her stripes gold.

"Ella!"

Suddenly Mum was in the garden beside me, all smart in her suit. "I need you inside now, Ella!"

"But I have to take more photos," I said.

"You'll have to do them later."

"But they're for Dad!"

Mum's jaw locked. "Look, love, I've got to get to work after I drop you at school. I said I'd be in by nine o'clock. If we're not in the car in five minutes, we'll all be late."

I trailed after her, back into the kitchen. "Put this on." She held out a blue cardigan. Its little gold buttons glinted.

"That's blue. The uniform's green."

"I've ordered your uniform. It's not my fault if it hasn't come yet. Look, love, this is quite … greenish." Mum locked the back door and shut the dishwasher.

"It's not green!" I said. "And it's for an old woman! I can't wear it."

Mum slammed down our new lunchboxes, glaring now. "Ella! Jack's in his home clothes too."

I looked over at Jack at the breakfast table, cereal spilling out of his grinning mouth.

"So what? Jack doesn't care what he wears," I said. "He gets filthy and covered in paint anyway."

"For your information, that *old woman's* cardigan's mine," Mum snapped. "And it's all we've got. You've got to wear something."

"Or be a nudie," Jack suggested.

I lunged at him, but Mum stepped in front of me. "In the car, both of you, this minute."

Her voice had a sob in it. "I'm tired of this rudeness, Ella. It's time you helped. It's hard enough…"

I pulled on her ugly cardigan. Hot little pinpricks started nipping me.

I rubbed my wrist backwards and forwards along the top of the kitchen chair. Stupid first day. Stupid clothes. We should never have come here.

✗

I followed the office lady down the wide echoey corridors into Willow class and stood while my new teacher, Mr Hales, introduced me. "This is Ella, everyone. Let's all try to make her feel really welcome."

Willow class. Green and grey. Heads and faces. Eyes studying me.

I pulled my cuffs down over my red, itchy hands.

My mouth wouldn't smile at all, like a person in an old photo.

Mr Hales seemed the friendliest person here. He had spiky blond hair and a pierced eyebrow. I peeped at the place where the ring went in. "Now let's see where there's a space." He pointed to an empty seat at the front. "Why don't you sit next to Stiggy."

I sat.

The boy beside me made an evil grin. "Your jumper's the wrong colour!"

✗

Playtime. The playground was massive. I hung upside down on the monkey bars in case Moor Lane School looked better the other way up, but it didn't. It was safer round the edge. Some people are edge people in playgrounds. Popular people go where they want and they are often in the middle, like colourful fish swimming in the sea. I was a grey fish. An edge fish.

I watched one girl called Lydia who was surrounded by girls the whole time, linking arms with each other and whispering. She was all glossy brown hair, clips and clasps. Polished. Her laugh sounded like a song, little notes up and up. When she laughed, one of her friends would do the laugh too, as if they were saying, "Wow, Lydia, you are the best entertainment on the planet." That's how it felt. I tried joining in the laughing when they were standing near but those girls just turned and stared, goofy-eyed. "What's so funny?" said the faces. "You don't fit."

They were right. "I'm sorry," I said, and moved away.

I had always had Grace. We met when we started at Nursery. Albatrosses find their friend for life and if their friend dies, they stay on their own. Albatrosses don't have to go to school. Grace had an older sister and a cat. Her mum was at home a lot because she taught piano and looked after Grace's grandma. They had a big garden and we used to play out there all the time, because she and her sister had a summerhouse-shed thing with actual rugs and cushions and her mum let them do anything they wanted. I couldn't have a summerhouse like Grace because Jack would have wrecked it and Mum would have made us tidy it up.

Me being on my own without Grace today hurt like bare feet outside in winter. I was in another country, where no one spoke the same language, even though they seemed to.

If a person could make a relative with a wish, maybe press a button or something like that, I would have chosen Grace as my sister. Even if I had to keep Jack, at least I'd have her as well.

I looked around the faces in Willow class, wishing Grace's face was among them – like suddenly she would be there. "I decided to come and live here. I'm actually your long-lost sister – no one told us."

Mum's awful cardigan made everything worse. It was not a bit green. Mum needed her eyes testing. *Over here, look, new girl, in the stupid cardigan!*

If only they'd let me keep my lovely new phone. I'd hardly stopped playing with the brilliant camera. I had put Grace's number in and texted her.

Hi Grace. There's no one here like you. Miss you lots. Ella

But the lady in the office told me I had to hand in my phone to her every day and collect it at the end of school.

When we had reading, everyone got moved around and I was put next to Bryony. She was weird. She kept frantically waving, but she hardly ever stayed in her seat until a grown-up helper came to sit next to her and tried to persuade her to work. She sat so close to me, nudging up nearer and nearer as if she hadn't got her own seat. And she talked all the time. I could hardly hear the teacher. Then she started stroking my pencil case. "It's furry!" she shrilled. "It could be alive…"

I ended up shoving it back in my bag.

Wasn't there anyone else on their own? Another pair person, like me? I checked the room secretly. Everyone had their special friend, that person to laugh with. Nobody smiled over at me. No one needed a new friend; I was an extra; a boring new person. They would look at me if they wanted me … and none of them were looking at me.

And then, at the back, hunched over a table, I noticed a dark-haired girl on her own. I sneaked looks at her. She looked back at me with tired eyes. Maybe she was watching me too. When we were doing art, making our own Van Gogh portraits, Mr Hales said we could sit where we liked. I clutched my bag to my chest, stood up and walked over so the girl would see me. I smiled. She stared up at me, gloomy-eyed. Then she bent, collected her bag and spread her things right across the desk as if she was saving that space for someone else.

I'd been wrong. She didn't want to know me. I stood there like a lemon until Mr Hales told me to sit next to that irritating Stiggy boy again. "Van Gogh cut off his ear," he whispered. "I'm going to draw me with only one ear." He grinned. "You could draw you with no nose."

He was just like my brother!

"Go away and fall off a cliff," I said, rubbing my wrist against the edge of the desk.

But at least that boy had talked to me.

I was rubbish at being new.

On a scrap of paper, at home time, I tried making myself a 'to-do' list the way Mum always did, just to look busy.

1. Get a green jumper NOW.
2. Get a plain black school bag.
3. Find a pencil case with NO KITTENS.
4. Shoes – brown lace-ups are a DISASTER. Maybe if some paint fell on them. All these girls have nice shoes – shiny or with flaps or studs or buckles.
5. Find a real friend who doesn't make out my pencil case is alive or suggest I cut off my nose!

✗

Mum collected me. She was picking up Jack anyway.

I exploded the minute the car door swung shut. "I have to get the right uniform. I CAN'T GO BACK IN THERE IN THIS CARDIGAN!"

Mum stopped at the traffic lights. "Well, actually, I did notice…"

But Jack interrupted, yelling out, as usual. "There's a boy in my class who's got a pencil case with engines."

Mum smiled. "Has he, Jack?"

"And the pens inside have faces."

Jack was munching crisps. Why did he get crisps?

I snatched the packet. "I am trying to talk about my uniform!" I shouted.

"Ella, that was unkind. Jack's allowed to tell me about his day too!" snapped Mum. "What's got into you? You promised you'd try harder when I let you have the phone." She sighed. "Look, love, I've seen an advert for a second-hand school uniform in the shop window of the supermarket."

"Can we go there now?"

"Not this minute. We'll have tea and drop Jack at his new football training."

"But we *will* go today? I don't care what it's like; we have to buy it!"

Chapter 2
Number 13

Dear Dad,

I hope you are not sad.

I'm going to tell you about our new house. It's number 74 Ash Grove. Everything is tidy and all the boxes are empty now, even though we only got here last week. There's a bedroom each. Mine is yellow. Mum let me choose the paint. There's a fluffy grey cat who comes to visit us. I can see her in the garden. What can you see out of your window?

Jack and me are at Moor Lane School.

Grandma sent me an iPhone and the camera is so fun.

Mum says her new job makes her very tired. Have you got lots to do?

I'm sending one photo of the cat and one of the new house. Jack wants you to have the picture he drew as well – he says it's a tiger.

I have to print photos with proper photo paper and it takes ages!!!

Love, Ella

Mum and I stood outside number 13. The house was the corner one at the end of our road. "We do not buy at the door" and "no callers" said all the stickers on the front door. It opened about three centimetres when Mum pressed the bell.

When I first saw a girl on the step, I thought she must be much older than me because she looked about ten feet tall – dark hair, grey tracksuit, bare feet. But then I recognised her from my class. It was the girl who sat on her own at the back, the gloomy-eyed one who had put her bag up on the desk. Mr Hales had called her Molly.

Just my luck: the unfriendliest person.

Molly must have recognised me too, but she just looked down at the steps. "What is it?" she mumbled.

"We came about the jumper," said Mum, adding, "Is it you that's selling it?"

Molly scowled. "Just one moment." She disappeared back inside.

"Well, she's obviously not going to ask us in," whispered Mum.

A wave of sadness hit me. I remembered Grace. When Dad was gone, I sat all day in her summerhouse hugging her furry ladybird cushion and she brought biscuits and squash and she made me a card that said "O Ella, I'm rely sorry".

Molly's house was smaller than ours. The curtains were drawn upstairs, even though it wasn't dark outside. The front room looked gloomy too, with what looked like boxes piled up against the window.

Molly slid out through the front door and thrust a carrier bag into my arms. "That's all of it," she said flatly. "There are shirts I grew out of too. No point keeping things when you don't need them."

When I took it out, her jumper looked very old. It smelled old too, dank and musty.

But it was the right green.

"You'll need to try it on, Ella," Mum said brightly.

"What, here?" *You want me to try on clothes outside someone's house?*

"Don't start," muttered Mum, holding my gaze. I knew what that meant – *Don't you dare argue … otherwise no jumper.*

"They'll fit; I grew out of them," Molly said. "You're small."

How *rude!* "Well, you're *massive*," I nearly said. And it was true; Molly's arms looked so lanky and giraffe-like – they stuck right out of the sleeves of the grey tracksuit top she had on – she might as well have sold that to us too.

I pulled off my hoody and pulled on the manky jumper.

"It's only for a while." Mum ran her hand over a place where the sleeve had been mended in a brownish kind of colour, "until the office gets your new ones." Mum sighed. "Is your mum in?"

Molly flinched, shook her head. "No!"

"Mol!" A faint woman's voice called from inside the house.

Molly froze.

"Molly!" Louder.

"I have to... go in," she said and she disappeared back inside.

"How strange," Mum said.

Mum's phone went. "It's my office. I won't be a sec, love." She walked back down to the gate.

"But, Mum..."

"Ask how much?" Mum called, before talking animatedly into her phone.

Why did Mum always dash off?

I felt something tickling my ankle. I looked down and jumped back. A rabbit had come out of the house. A really big one was snuffling around my shoes. Like in *Alice in Wonderland*.

My first thought was to grab my phone. Take a picture. But he could get run over out here. Silly thing.

I gently nudged him with my foot. "In you go, come on." I pushed the front door, whooshing him back in.

Shadows seemed to close around me.

I looked slowly up.

Molly's hall was a mountain.

Chapter 3
Rabbits and
Mountains

Hi Dad,
Here's a photo of my new bedroom for you. Mum says it's very yellow – a bit of a shock – but I like it.
It will be like good weather all year.
Love, Ella

You know when you have a doll's house and some mean brother tips it on its side and all the little things tumble and fall? Well, that was Molly's house. Someone seemed to have shaken it so hard that some of the furniture had fallen over. But there was far more furniture than normal houses too – enough for ten houses. I could see wardrobes, chairs, sculptures, an actual sink in the middle of the hall. And machinery and packages and jugs and blankets and… well, just everything. The smell was bad. Cabbage-y.

Rabbits and cabbages. Weird!

I shouldn't be in here.

But I still wanted to get a photo of that rabbit. Where was he? I pulled out my phone, opened the camera, set off. Past the sink, a chest of drawers, basket of clothes, a table on its side, through into the darkened front room.

More odd stuff! A rocking horse, a pottery pot… There it was: the whisk of white. Strong back legs leaping. The white rabbit. *Click… click.*

No wonder the room looked so dark from outside.

A white bobtail disappeared into a tunnel of wooden furniture legs… *click.* A rolled-up carpet.

A piano and, yes, a rocking horse on top. A picture on top of a suitcase on top of an armchair on top of...

Rustle...

Something stirred. "Molly?" A little breathy voice. A head turning.

I looked down. The side of a pale face with a dark cloak wrapped round. White fingers stretching out to me. A person!

I was back in the hallway in a flash and out the door, panting, shoving the phone in my pocket.

Feet came down the stairs. I stood on the front doorstep, swung round and felt eyes on me – Molly, only just behind. "Where's your mum. Has she gone?" she asked.

It was like a challenge, like, *have you lost her?*

"I... um... I mean, Mum got a phone call."

Molly's stern eyes rested on me.

I made my face blank. My eyes slid down to a pair of mud-crusted green PE socks, dangling from her hand. "I grew out of these too," she said in her flat dead voice. "Ten pounds for all of it."

I nodded frantically. "Thank you... I mean, OK. I'll get the money off Mum." Thank goodness, just then Mum appeared at the garden gate.

Ten pounds was handed over. Molly retreated back inside.

"Nice to meet you!" called Mum as the front door slammed shut.

I shook my head at Mum. "Why did you leave me?"

I took off, running up the road. It felt so good to be away from there.

Mum caught up. "Ella! Slow down. I want to talk to you. Did you know that girl from school?"

"I think she's in my class. She's called Molly. She's weird."

"Maybe she's shy."

"She's rude."

"Well, at least we got your jumper. Let's give it a wash. It is second-hand."

"No, Mum. I need it for tomorrow."

Mum frowned. "All right. Well, that's another thing ticked off."

She let us in. She had put up a little cupboard in the hall with hooks for all the keys and she handed me hers to hang up.

"I want to cycle to school. Can I?" I asked.

"It seems rather early days. I'll think about it," Mum said, disappearing into the study.

I stared at the keys with their neat labels ... Back Door ... Bikes ... Spare Front ... One key ring looked familiar. I unhooked it. A yellow and blue snapping crocodile, hard and shiny. It was Dad's; I'd given it to him for his birthday. I remembered him saying how much he loved the snapping crocodile; he would never lose his keys again. I twisted the key off, hung it back on the hook and put the key ring in my pocket.

I wiped my eyes and took my shoes off.

That evening, after tea, I flicked through the pictures on my phone, looking for the rabbit. Most of them were of Molly's strange house. The rabbit was only good in one of them, leaping away from the camera.

Molly's house looked like nobody cared.

At least I'd got my jumper, even if it did look old and worn.

Even though only a few hours had passed, I felt as if I must have dreamed Molly's strange house down the road ... like a place in a film.

Not real at all.

That evening, Mum came to say goodnight and

watched me while I soaked my hands.

"I saw you were writing to Dad again," she murmured.

I darted a look at her, my face flushing, and stopped swirling the oil around my fingers. "Have *you* written to him, Mum?"

Mum sighed. "You're not old enough to understand…"

"He won't know what we're doing." Words tumbled out. "I need to tell him about the house and school and…"

"I don't mind you writing." Mum's voice had gone firm and brisk. "Now, let's just leave it." She patted my hands dry, handed me my pot of cream and helped me rub it in. "I'm glad we've sorted out your uniform."

I climbed into bed and she kissed me. "And you're pleased with the phone? Grandma was determined to get you one."

"It's brilliant. I love it."

Mum was at my door. But then she stopped. "Just one thing. Let's not talk about what happened in Milton… with other people, I mean."

"Nobody?"

"I really can't discuss this, Ella. There's so many

new things to sort out." She came over and hugged me tightly. "We're going to be happy here: new school, my job... Please, love, don't argue." She flicked off my light. "Goodnight."

Chapter 4
Party Invite

Dear Dad,

There is a girl on our road called Molly and her house is a big mess because no one tidies it. Mum would call it a DISGRACE. Mum says I can cycle to school but not yet.

I think about you a lot at night. You know the creaky floorboards outside your bedroom and you pretending it was our own friendly ghost? In this house it's the water pipes – they clank at six o'clock in the morning and Mum says a rude thing and gets up.

Ella

The next day, Mr Hales smiled at me as I came in and took my place. He had changed his eyebrow ring for a black stud.

I fidgeted with the sleeves of Molly's old jumper in the warm classroom. My wrists were flaming red. I had scratched them badly in the night. The jumper felt prickly, but I didn't take it off. My white school shirt was short-sleeved; everyone would see. Horrid eczema.

"Where's your blue jumper?" Stiggy asked.

"A rabbit ate it," I said.

"Really?" Stiggy's eyebrows went up.

I rolled my eyes at him. "It's a joke!"

Molly was at the back again, bent over a notebook. She never talked to anyone and nobody talked to her. Like a piece of furniture, a girl-shaped grey table. At playtime, I stayed round the edge of the playground again, hanging off the railings, gazing up, trying to decide what kinds of animals the clouds looked like.

And then a face took the place of a cloud and Lydia was there, all smart, her chestnut hair scrunched in little clips that must have taken ages to do and bracelets on her wrists even though they weren't allowed. "Ella," she called. "You live near me. I've seen you. You've got a little brother in my sister's class."

My heart raced. Why had she come to talk to me? "His name's Jack," I said, all in a rush.

Lydia stayed there, looking at me. "Well, my sister Anna is a champion swimmer."

"Oh." I tried to look interested and pleased.

"See you got your uniform then?" Her eyes scanned me, like someone staring at things for sale in a shop they wouldn't usually visit.

I pulled down my cuffs. "It's from a girl in my road. Until my proper things arrive."

"Mmm," said Lydia, smiling. "You've changed your school bag too." Lydia's eyes were so big, they shined more than normal eyes.

"Yep."

She tossed her hair and the clips clicked. "I liked the kittens. Cute."

I tried to feel pleased. At least Lydia was being friendly. Wasn't she?

"Well, byeee!" she called, skipping away.

She wouldn't be back. I looked up at the clouds again and wished I could be up there on top of one: a girl in a cloud, lost in whirling smoke.

I kept trying to join conversations, then finding

myself standing alone. Boys wouldn't talk to me properly. In Milton, there'd always been loads of boys I could chat to, but these ones seemed to race off or laugh. The sun came out. I wandered and watched shouting people rushing around and calling for someone to pass them the ball. Molly was perched by the railings near me with a notebook on her knee. She didn't look up.

My eyes were always drawn back to Lydia because she was surrounded by so many laughing girls. Like a queen bee. And what was I, Ella Mackay? A new-bee? Imagine being in the middle of everyone. *Oh, ask Ella... Ella's so fun!*

At afternoon break, I watched people coming and going at the water fountain, like birds, head peck down, head peck up. A voice shouted my name. "Ella!" I saw Lydia swinging her legs on the monkey bars. "Come here!"

I hurried over and stretched my arms out to help Lydia jump down.

She gave me a smile, just like that, like a gift. "I'm going to Immy's after school," she said.

Suddenly I wanted desperately to go to Immy's too – even though I'd only just worked out which one she was – to curl up with a friend and watch

TV and play games and laugh... well, anything really.

"Does she live near here?"

Lydia smiled and pursed her lips together as if she had something hard to explain. "No, her mum's picking us up. We might go to a film..."

I knew what that meant. *It's all planned. You're not included. Buzz off!*

"Oh, well, bye then." I turned away.

But Lydia bobbed back beside me. The smile came on again. "I'm having a party next weekend, for my birthday."

My heart skipped. "Are you?" My voice sounded squeaky, too excited. I tried again. "Are you?" That sounded better.

"Saturday. Four thirty." Lydia was still smiling, fixing her big blue eyes on me. "And a sleepover."

"Four thirty," I repeated, as if it was a memory test.

Lydia skipped away and left me... on top of the world. An invitation. A party! But as soon as she had gone, worries started nagging at me. Had she invited me to the party just then? She wasn't telling me about her party just for something to chat about, was she?

All the rest of the day, I replayed what she'd said... *Saturday. Four thirty. Sleepover.* I kept gazing across the classroom. Would Lydia hand me a smart invitation? Then I'd know.

If you had taken a picture of me, you would have seen me concentrating and listening. I kept the green jumper on so no one would see the sore patches down my arms. I would blend in. I could blend. I'd be so blended I'd be... liquidised.

I hung round the edge of Lydia's group. I smiled whenever they smiled, laughed whenever they all seemed to be laughing. They all wore a woven blue and green bracelet Lydia had bought them on holiday. "Hey, Lydia did you know this?" one of them would call, or, "I heard this hilarious thing..." The group was a mixture of different girls; so complicated. There was Sophie who was nearly always with Lydia. Then there was Hannah and Rachel, and then Zing and Immy. Immy was always rushing back from being in a sports team, but she was the most smiley, which must be a good thing. Rachel actually talked to me sometimes. Hannah and Zing giggled a lot. Sophie sort of looked past me, as if she was waiting for someone else.

I waited for my party invitation, but nothing

happened and nobody mentioned it.

✗

Mum had arranged for me to do art club after school on Mondays because I liked art. Jack would be doing football practice. There was a special art loft at the top of the school, in the roof space, with beams stretching up and the sun pouring in through the huge roof windows. The teacher was a proper artist. The first surprise was the radio playing in the corner and the voice of the DJ announcing songs.

A woman with a mass of white hair under a stripy band appeared out of a dark alcove. "Just emptying the kiln," she said in a warm friendly voice. "Spread yourselves. You need room to breathe!" She saw me and came over. "Our new girl. This is not an ordinary club. We have two important rules. DON'T BE HORRID and DON'T SCOFF ALL THE BISCUITS. Welcome to art club, Ella."

There were twelve of us. Each person took a table to themselves. All around us were interesting things to get ideas from and strange objects to draw – shells, costumes, driftwood and puppets, a skeleton in a bowler hat in the corner.

The club had started several weeks before so the others were used to finding their own things.

"OK, Ella, this is not a telling-off club. This is not an all-doing-the-same club. This is a WHAT-DO-I-REALLY-LOVE?-OK-I'll-do-that club," said our teacher. "What do you want to do – make something, create an image?"

Miss Denby looked like a hen – rounded, not very tall, her white hair scrunched and flying out at the sides. I stared at the messy paint stains on her shirt and decided I liked her.

I held out a photo of waves rushing into a cave.

"Did you take this yourself?" Miss Denby asked.

"Yes."

"Great!"

Miss Denby suggested I made a collage of my photo using tiny little bits of torn-up paper from magazines, matching colours and laying them glued next to each other until the white paper underneath couldn't be seen any more. She left me to start.

A few minutes passed. The door crashed open.

Chapter 5
A Bird with a
Large Beak!

Dear Dad,

I've been watching a squirrel. Sometimes it dashes up and down but other times it goes frozen still. Maybe it knows I'm watching and wants to pretend to be a bit of tree. It doesn't understand that it's easy to see. Do you ever wish that you could be so still and frozen that nobody would see you?

Ella

"Sorry I'm late again, miss. Mum was dropping off my equipment." It was Lydia.

"Just sort yourself out, Lydia," called Miss Denby.

"Ella! You're here!" Lydia plonked herself right beside me and put down a large wooden box, a bit like a briefcase, and began unloading it. "I can't let you borrow any of my things – they cost two hundred pounds. I'll tell you about them, though... *This* is a kind of smudger. *This* is very expensive ink that Mum has to order. She says I'm unusually creative..."

Being next to Lydia in art club was like having the TV on in the house except that every now and then I had to agree with her or she would ask a question and wait for an answer. But mostly she just prattled. Like a bird... with a very large beak! "This is so fun, Miss Denby... You're my favourite teacher, miss... Miss, when's your birthday? Which is your car in the car park...? If I make this blue then yellow, it looks wrong. Aww...! Can we have the radio louder?"

Miss Denby seemed used to her. "Lydia Sheridan, you're like a wind-up toy. Just give us all a bit of peace," she said.

"I love this song." Lydia started singing. "You're my only-eeeee—"

"Lydia, that's too loud," Miss Denby called.

"Can I hum then?"

"Lydia, everyone else is getting on with their work except you."

Lydia flicked ink on her picture. "That's ruined now." She flicked some more. "Actually, I think it looks better." She grabbed my arm and hugged me to her. "Art club is perfect now you're here."

I tore off more bits of coloured magazine to add to my pile.

"You and me are going to bring sweets every week – Miss Denby won't care. She gets cross," whispered Lydia, "but she's a pussycat."

"A pussycat with ears who can hear every word you say, young lady," Miss Denby said.

Lydia smiled. Then her face changed. "You haven't forgotten about my party, have you, Ella?" she asked sharply. Her eyebrows went up. She tutted. "Well, are you coming or aren't you? Ask your mum."

"I ... I ... I, yes, I'll ask her... Thank you," I said.

Lydia poked me hard. "Funny Ella," she giggled.

"Thank you," I said again, giggling too.

Hi Grace – my room is yellow. I'm gonna miss your birthday 😞
Who are you sitting next to?
Hi Ella – I'm sitting with Abbi. She says hi.
Hi Grace – A cat comes in our garden – a bit like Percy but fatter. Can you come and visit one day?

✗

At home that evening, Mum cleaned and piled up the towels while I soaked my hands and rubbed all the different creams into the hot, irritated skin.

"So, have you made any friends yet?" she asked.

"I think so…"

"And you're getting used to it?"

I nodded.

"And the lessons. Maths? And writing?"

"The work's fine, Mum."

"You mentioned somebody … Lydia?" Mum held out a towel and folded it over my fingers. I love that moment when the itching stops.

"She invited me to her party next Saturday so she must think I'm all right."

Mum laughed. "Of course she does, love. That's great." She frowned. "You don't look very happy about it."

"It's just … I don't really know her. I don't really know anyone."

I thought about Grace's text and found my eyes filling with tears. Maybe Grace had found a proper friend already.

"I know it's hard, but just be yourself, love," Mum was saying.

I didn't say it to Mum, but I wasn't sure what 'being myself' meant.

When she'd gone, I drew a picture of Lydia and stuck a crown on her head with the title Lydia's Court Rules.

1. Lydia decides everything. You're lucky if she chooses you.
2. She can go off people but you can't go off her.
3. Lydia has nice things, especially hair and art things.
4. If I'm lucky, I'll get to be her third-best friend. Exciting!

I switched off the light again and made myself think about all the photos I could take of those strange objects in the art room.

I thought about Grace and the days we had

spent decorating the wall in her summerhouse last summer with snippets from magazines, sketches and photos, and telling her everything, even the hardest things. Grace felt very real when the light was off – so real I sat up and texted her again.

Grace – are you OK? Did you get my message about coming to see me for a weekend or something? Can you ask your mum? I really want to see you.

I lay back in bed and tried to imagine Lydia being in the garden with me instead of Grace, or, sometimes, me being the one she chose to sit next to in class rather than Sophie or Rachel. I thought about us laughing together in art club.

But Lydia was a loud person. And, anyway, how would I ever get to be her first choice? I felt like a person in a queue, but at the back. Lydia seemed to like me but she didn't know me. But she had invited me to her party.

School got easier as that first week went on. Willow class were OK. I liked Mr Hales, especially when he played his guitar for us. Stiggy was actually quite funny and rude, and there were other children who hated PE as much as I did. I couldn't help scratching the backs of my legs and rubbing them against the metal edges of the school chairs.

We went to a doctor's surgery.

"How is your new school, Ella?" the doctor asked. "Have you made some friends? Are you happy?"

I stared at the colours in his beard. I kept nodding. My head could have fallen off I was nodding so much.

We came out with bags and bags of new creams and Mum kept saying no one would look at my hands.

I loved taking pictures with the new camera on my phone: by the river, apples in a bowl, our bikes leaning in the shed.

And, all week long, I felt little ripples of excitement and worry each time I remembered. I was going to Lydia's party!

Chapter 6
Lydia's Party

Hi Dad,

Jack has a new friend called Felix and they are always being superheroes loudly!!!!

Moor Lane is a very big school with masses of corridors. Did I tell you my teacher is Mr Hales? He's funny and he plays the guitar and sings songs about Willow class. Last week, he sang, "All the kids from Moor Lane School fell into a swimming pool", and we all made up extra bits. Do you remember singing stupid words to Jack's music in the car, like "I've got a hamster, you've got broccoli, we've all got marmalade, yeah!" I suddenly thought about that. I still don't know anybody who sings like you.

Love, Ella

Saturday came. I took ages choosing a pair of tiny sparkly blue earrings in town. I'd noticed Lydia had pierced ears. I pictured her opening the yellow wrapping, saying, "Oh, Ella, they're the best present I've had!"

I walked round to Lydia's house, loaded up with a sleeping bag and overnight stuff and rang the doorbell. I stood by a big pink flowering bush in the front garden, listening to laughter ringing out from inside.

The doorbell played a tune.

Sophie came to let me in wearing a blue spangly dress. "Ella!" she screamed. She held out her arms like a sleepwalker. Did she want a hug? I stepped uncertainly towards her but she just waved her hands about and giggled, rushing away down a wide hallway that smelled of polish, calling, "You're late. Everyone's out the back."

Late?

I caught sight of my reflection in a gold-edged mirror: red straight hair just past my shoulders, small pale face. I should have been in a dress more like Sophie's, instead of my summer trousers and long-sleeved T-shirt with embroidered owls. Mum liked girls to wear practical clothes. I lined up my brown shoes next to lots of bright party ones. Beautiful. I must ask Mum again about shoes.

I found everybody in the conservatory at the back of the kitchen. Little shrieks of hellos. Lydia was stretched out on a long pink sofa with girls lounged around her. There must have been at least twenty. "Ella! Just put the present in the pile on the piano," she called.

"Oh, Ella, you're here," said Immy. "Weren't you free at two thirty then?"

The room went quiet. I stared around at them all.

Lydia smiled. "We've got ages," was all she said.

Two thirty? Lydia had definitely said four thirty. Why had she invited me two hours after everyone else?

"Oh, you brought a sleeping bag. Well done," called Lydia's mum, appearing from behind a giant pink frosted cake. "How about all you girls go out on the trampoline while we clear up?"

I looked at them all stretching out their fingers, full of little admiring cries. A lady in a white apron was packing away little bright bottles. I could smell the acid tang. Nail varnish – they'd all had their nails decorated in bright colours and designs.

I made myself grin but the smile felt tight on my face, wrong on my mouth.

As they all disappeared outside, Lydia came up to me. "I knew you wouldn't want your nails done," she said. "I've told the others that they won't catch your disease just from touching you, but if you have nail varnish on, people will look at your hands more … won't they, Ella?"

I flushed, a whole tight ball of misery rising inside me.

Lydia pursed her lips. She was being kind. "Aw, this must happen to you such a lot," she said.

Of course everyone was bound to have noticed how bad my hands looked; so flaky and red raw. But I'd never been to a nail varnish party. And now I never would.

Tears brimmed in my eyes. I blinked them back. I stood stupidly. *Do not cry in front of her. Don't!*

I joined the others outside and watched them bounce on Lydia's trampoline.

"No more than six at a time!" Lydia's dad shouted.

There always seemed to be six every time I tried

to have a go. I took loads of photos of Sophie and Hannah and Rachel doing star jumps. It was so hard to catch them leaping high, mid jump. I did get to go on the trampoline eventually, with some girls from Lydia's dance class. They were doing forward rolls and amazing jumps and I got off and took some photos of them too. We ate a huge tea and watched two scary films, all hiding behind plush stripy cushions. Everyone grabbed their friends when the zombies attacked and although nobody grabbed me I liked screaming.

Rachel flopped down beside me and held out the bowl of popcorn, laughing "That was so scary!" Rachel was a quiet kind of person. We discovered we were reading the same book. Immy talked to me too, about the school football team.

Most of the girls left after the film. Lydia's special friends from school were going to be sleeping in the loft, her dad said. That included me. When we went up there, I felt really pleased all over again that Lydia had invited me; it was decorated like a grotto with little sparkly lights and orange lava lamps in the corners that glooped. While we stretched out all the bedrolls and mattresses,

Lydia told each person where they were going to sleep and I really didn't mind sleeping next to the door; I could get out easily to go to the loo. I felt safer there too; it was nearer home, for getting out. So, that was good.

I put my pyjamas on in a shiny green bathroom and wished they were more interesting or had film characters on. I didn't have slippers, so I just put my socks back on. I tried not to mind that my sleeping bag was just one of our brown family camping ones.

Lydia told everyone to sit. "Each of us is going to tell a secret." Her eyes flashed. "It's got to be a juicy one that no one else knows."

Lydia's eyes were like an Egyptian cat's in the orange glow: so big and blue and staring.

Panic hit me. Think about a secret… My own family secret filled my head. Mum had said not to tell anyone. I thought of Mum saying over and over "It's no one's business but ours," and me promising, saying "Don't worry, Mum." I flushed. I felt as if the truth must be written on my face. What could I say that wasn't our secret, Mum's, Jack's and mine?

All the others were giggling, just like they had

at the film, and there was a frenzy of whispers. I needed to think of something else private or important. My best friend from my old school is called Grace? No, that wasn't a proper secret.

Lydia pointed to the one who was going to speak. She picked Sophie first.

"You all know mine," Sophie said, and everyone burst out laughing except me, but I caught up and laughed loudly even though I had no idea why.

"If it's about you and James, that doesn't count," said Lydia like a game show host.

"I smashed an ornament at my nan's and hid it behind the fridge and it's still there!" Sophie giggled.

Gasps. "That's really bad…! What was it?"

"An ugly bird. I was only five."

Murmurs of sympathy.

"I copied Angelina's history homework and got a commendation and she didn't," Immy said.

Big laugh.

"I hid in the loos to miss the maths test," Rachel said.

My hands went sweaty. I stared at all the grinning faces. Nobody had said they couldn't think of a secret and almost everyone had said one now.

"I ate my sister's Easter egg and told my mum and dad that she'd left it on the bus," said Zing.

I smiled then. Maybe I could think of a Jack thing. That would be all right. Eating sweets from the big tin at Christmas and blaming it on him? That was a great one. But, all at once, Lydia's finger was pointing at *me*.

Chapter 7
Secret Time

Dear Dad,

Is your food nice? If Mum lets me come and visit one day, I could bring you some cake. Mum always makes Jack and me eat very sensible food, which is not nice, but it will make us live for a long time. Do you remember our Pizza Jellybeana nights? Do you remember your marshmallow and liquorice one? I'm sending you a picture of me and Jack in the garden and a joke photo I made with lots of different things to go on pizza. Which is the odd one out? Shall I send you Blu-tac for sticking them up?

Love, Ella

All those eyes, staring. My Jack idea went out of my head. *Think. Quickly. Something bad or wrong.*

"Last week I went inside a house that was so messy the piles of things made walls," I told them. "You wouldn't even be able to walk around in there."

A few people shrugged. "Maybe they were having a clear-out," someone suggested. "That's just being untidy."

"My bedroom's like that," Sophie said.

"Were there rats?" asked Immy.

"No... not rats," I said.

How could I explain? I took my mind back to that house where Molly lived... to that rabbit leading me. "There were towers of things. There was a piano with a rocking horse on top and furniture in the middle of a room with a fireplace and a sofa on its side and cupboards and guitars and sculptures."

Now they were all listening. Now their faces looked like, "Mmm, how odd..."

Everyone joined in. "Imagine if there were so many piles of things inside your house, you got lost."

"I wish my sister would get lost!"

"Like a maze."

"Where was it? Near here?" Lydia's bright eyes seemed to burrow inside me.

I rubbed my wrist on the frayed label of my sleeping bag.

"Come on. Does someone from school live there?"

I nodded, wriggling, gripping the zip, grating it against the skin. A cold squirming feeling started in my insides.

"Is this person in our class?"

"You're making this up," Sophie said.

"Is it Molly Gardener?" Lydia asked.

The giggles stopped.

"Is it *her* house?"

"She is so odd... she never invites anyone," Hannah said.

A ripple of conversation began and this time I could join in.

"Nobody ever invites *her*."

"I heard she went to Georgie's party ages ago and she gave her a scarf as a present that was second-hand with a hole in."

"She's weird."

"She didn't talk to me," I said. The squirming feeling got stronger – a seasick kind of dread. "She just wanted money. She just wanted us to go away."

In the shadows, behind the bubbling lamps, Molly's stern face with its curling black hair and dark eyes seemed to watch me... that tall serious girl listening.

"Did you see anyone else?" Immy asked.

"Doesn't she live at number 13?" asked Hannah.

The figure all curled up I'd seen in Molly's living room, with the long white fingers, sprang into my mind. The strange front room in Molly's house and then, looming out, the headless thing from the graveyard in the film we'd just watched.

"Imagine living in a really properly haunted house though..." Hannah said.

"Maybe Molly's a werewolf," Zing said. "Maybe she turns all hairy when there's a full moon."

"Yeah."

Some faces grinned, teased; mouths and eyes lit up in the glooping orange light.

"Takes off her head," Immy said, "waits for you."

"You're creeping me out!" Rachel said. "Put

the lights on."

"No!" Lydia said. "No, it's better like this."

My cold squirming feeling about Molly seemed to fade away. And my family secret was safe too. I laughed. It was fun. Everyone was just making things up.

"Imagine if a cat wandered inside," Zing said.

"It would starve," said Immy.

"Yeah," everyone echoed.

"It would stagger all the way up the piled-up things," Sophie said.

Immy laughed. "Yeah, there's the poor cat going, 'I'll never get to the other side of this stupid house – there's an even bigger pile in *this* room!'"

Lydia jumped up. "Come on."

She made us all drag our sleeping bags into one big mountain. Sophie did an impression of a staggering cat trying to get up it, then we all tried to climb it and slid off.

After that, the secrets turned into stupid secrets.

"My secret is I sing in the bath."

"I saw Jessica Branson at the cinema with a boy."

"That's her brother."

"Oh... oh well."

✗

"I liked your secret best," Lydia said when we were brushing our teeth. "It was... different."

Delight rose inside me.

I pulled out my special handwash and quickly squirted my hands and rinsed them.

Lydia opened a pot of blue jelly stuff and rubbed some on her face. "How come Molly let you in, though?"

I hesitated. My breath felt tight. "I was buying the uniform she was selling," I said. "What's that cream you're putting on?"

Lydia didn't seem to have heard. She began wiping her face with a cloth. "So Molly actually *asked* you in?"

I thought of the rabbit and shooing it back inside. Molly hadn't invited me in. She hadn't been friendly at all.

"So clever," Lydia went on, "getting invited into Molly's house. Nobody else has ever been to Molly's." She soaked a white pad in some liquid and rubbed it around her eyes.

Lydia seemed to do so many things to her face.

"I am disappointed, though," she said. "Ella...

really disappointed… in you." Her hands stopped moving.

"Are you?" My voice trembled. Lydia seemed to be staring right inside me.

"There's something that you're not telling me. I can see it in your face." Her voice had a harsh slicing tone. "How can I be your friend if you don't tell me, Ella? I let you come to my sleepover."

A huge rush of hot feelings in my head, like electric wire, burning. "I promised Mum." The words leaked out of me. And then the shame of it. My hand flew to my mouth. "No… no, I can't!" I stared into the sink where the soap had left white foam round the sides.

Lydia's arm came round my shoulder. "Poor, poor Ella," she said very gently. "Everyone's got a secret."

"Have they?" I hiccoughed.

"Of course." Her face snapped back to relaxed, chatty Lydia. "I… I love your name… 'Bella' means 'beautiful' in Italian. My mum told me. *Ciao, bella!*" she sang. "Hello, beautiful! See these cat faces on my pyjamas? I've got dog ones too."

She rinsed out her mouth.

I rubbed some cream on my hands and tried to smile. I should be able to think of a name for her too. I definitely should. But I could only think of 'Lyd' like a lid for a pen or a pan.

"Can we go back to the others now?" I asked.

"My funny girl!" she giggled. "Come on."

Up in the loft again, we all threw the pillows and had a midnight feast and… it was like I was part of everything. We all chatted for ages, so long that I fell asleep even before Lydia's mum came up to tell everyone off and woke me again.

"Friends for ever, Ella Bella," Lydia whispered to me, as I left the next morning.

"Yes… I mean, thank you," I whispered back, grinning at her as she moved to hug the next person.

Hi Grace – I miss bike ballet. This cat comes in our garden – I've called him Smokey. Did you ask your mum if you can come and stay?

Hi Ella – everyone says hi. I'm glad you got a cat.

Hi Grace – I haven't got a cat. It's not mine.

Say hi to Abbi for me.

Hi Ella – I taught bike ballet to Abbi. She's really good! We're on holiday next weekend and Abbi's coming too. Can't wait!

Hi Grace – did you ask your mum about coming to see me?

Hi Grace – I might be back at Christmas. I could come and see you.

Hi Grace – are you on your holiday now? Why don't you answer?

Chapter 8
A Present

Dear Dad,

My best friend Lydia invited me to her party and it was AMAZING – the cake had pink and white mice all over it and it tasted of strawberries. (I only ate a small bit and I was fine.) Here is a selfie of the loft with all the sleepover people. Immy is the one near the front and Zing and Rachel are next to the big lamp. We watched two scary films. Argh!

Lydia likes art – same as me!

Ella

On Monday, at school, Lydia handed me a little envelope. The card inside read "thanx for your gift" and then a space where she'd written, "Earrings – cool!"

Everyone already had their places in Willow class. I didn't mind. I just had to keep my pencils and things away from Bryony so she didn't steal them. I'm sure that's where my sharpener with the cats went. Bryony wriggled things to the edge of the table and flicked them down into her bag. I saw her. I kept catching Lydia's eye all that day and she held on to my gaze each time. I kept wondering about texting Grace again. Grace going on holiday with this person called Abbi. I couldn't remember her at all. Maybe she met her at Sea Scouts. No, that couldn't be right; she said she was sitting next to her. If I was still there, would we be in a three?

At lunchtime, when I was sitting on my own on the wall, Lydia's voice rang out. "Now, where is my Ella Bella?"

Her whole group appeared around me: Immy was chasing Zing, Sophie was arm in arm with Rachel.

"Ella!" Lydia pulled out a carrier bag. "Look

what I've got for you."

"Did you leave something behind at the sleepover?" Rachel asked.

"I don't think so," I said.

"It's present time," Lydia said. "Silly!"

She opened the bag and held up the sparkly pink shoes she had worn at her birthday party on Saturday. "Ta-da!" The air filled with gasps.

Lydia did a little dance step, twirling. She sang me her laugh. "You love them, don't you?"

"I... I... yes," I said. "They're really... they're nice. But it's not my birthday."

"Who cares?"

"Why are you giving those to Ella?" Immy asked.

"None of your business, Miss Nosy-pants," Lydia said.

I realised my mouth was wide open so I shut it.

"Well, try them on," Lydia said impatiently.

I scrabbled to undo my laces and dropped a shoe and pulled the pretty sparkly one over my school sock.

"Perfect," said Lydia.

Soon I had both of them on and Lydia was making me turn round so the others could see.

The shoes felt tight round my toes but I didn't care. I looked from surprised face to surprised face. Proper party shoes. Mum would never have bought me shoes like these. Lydia's present was a miracle.

"Why are you giving Ella your shoes?" Immy asked again.

Lydia shook her head, crossly. "Ella is new. I just want her to have them. I knew they would be right for her. And they are."

Everyone stood admiring my feet. I pointed my toes. She had chosen me.

"Anyway, Mum's buying me some new ones," Lydia added.

"Oh, right."

Everyone seemed to melt away after that.

I didn't care if Lydia was getting new shoes. Nobody had ever given me anything so beautiful. Could I actually walk home in them? I wondered.

When I collected my phone from the office at the end of the day, I seemed to be floating in pink shoe land. Mum had told me to walk back on my own today. I was already at the school gates and heading home with a great big smile on my face when a voice beside me said, "I knew you'd love them!"

It was Lydia again.

"Isn't anyone meeting you?" I asked.

But Lydia was sliding her arm through mine. "I told Mum I was walking back with my new friend. You can show me your house. I like learning where people live. I keep it all stored inside my head. Come on!"

So, Lydia walked home with me. The shoes went on feeling like tiny cheese graters round the edges of my big toes but I didn't care. Lydia told me about her sister being a champion swimmer and always being dragged along to watch, and her mum being a buyer for a big shop, and in no time at all we were at my front door. Lydia stopped talking and looked up at my house. I wasn't sure what to do. But when I had rung the bell, Lydia said, "Well, go on then, ask me in, Ella!" just as Mum opened the door, so, of course, I did.

We had juice and biscuits and Mum smiled and said, "See you girls in a while," and "How lovely to have a friend over."

"I have to see your room," Lydia said, leaping up. "Come on." I followed her out and up the stairs. "It's so yellow," she said, throwing herself down on my bed. "It's a lovely little room. Haven't you got a TV?" She walked around staring at everything and asking about my eczema creams and the pictures on my pinboard. She pointed to one of Grandma and Grandad, and I told her Grandad died last year. Then she cuddled my giant furry ladybird that Grace gave me. "It's like a big tummy!" She laughed. I took a photo of her holding it and she made me sit down next to her while I was still smiling and said, "You really love the shoes, don't you?"

"Yes," I said, because it was true.

She picked up the framed photo by my bed, from more than a year ago, when our family were still together. Mum, Dad, me and Jack all hugging and grinning in a café in Spain. "It's just you and your mum and your brother living here, isn't it?"

A hot pang of worry shot through me. My room seemed to shrink; Lydia and the ladybird were taking up the whole bed.

"Ella," she said, her voice soft beside me, "best friends tell each other everything."

"Do they?" My voice sounded all wobbly.

"You know they do, Ella. Look, how can I help you if you don't tell me? Think how much you like the shoes. I haven't given shoes to anyone else. That makes me your very special friend, Ella." She patted my arm. "If it's easier, you can not look at me. You'll feel better, you know, when you tell me."

In a flash the twisting panic in my stomach was back.

"It's your dad, isn't it?" I heard Lydia say. "Is this him?"

She was pointing at the photo. There was Dad all suntanned right in the middle with his arms round me and Jack. "He looks really nice." She stroked my arm.

A gate seemed to open inside me. "Mum doesn't want us to talk about him. I said I wouldn't." Tears started to drip. I watched them fall onto my lap and disappear into my trousers... little dark spots. "Mum'll be so cross," I heard myself say.

"This is what friends are for." Lydia snuggled up to me. "So, where is he?"

She was waiting, staring. The secret began coming from my mouth. "Dad... he's gone away."

"Has he? Aw..."

"For three years..."

"Three years! Mmm. Where then? Is he working... *He's not, is he?*"

"No... he's... he's, he's in a... a... prison."

Lydia let out a really big sigh. "Did he do a bad thing?"

Words poured out. "He took some money and then he lied about it."

Lydia patted my arm. "Never mind," she said. "My dad goes away for work and Mum says it's easier without him. She says she's too busy to sort him out."

All at once, Lydia was standing again. "I should go. Well done." She sounded like a teacher. "Well done, Ella. We won't tell the others about your secret. Whenever you want to talk about it, you've got me."

Chapter 9
What Friends
Are For

Dear Dad,

When you went away you only took a carrier bag. I've been wondering if you have enough clothes. Are you cold?

I saw a TV programme with an old prison in it and all the beds were in lines, like a hospital. Is your bed in a line?

Why won't they let you have the blu-tac? Tell them you really need it. Then, when you put my pictures up by your bed, your friends will say, "Oh, a new picture!"

I could send you a jumper. I know where the post office is. Just tell me.

Love, Ella

When she'd gone, I went back upstairs and wrote to Dad again. I felt as if I had hurt Dad somehow, but it was Mum who would be cross, if she knew. It was Mum who had asked me not to tell anyone. But Lydia seemed to sort of know... didn't she? She'd worked it out.

In the days after I told Lydia, when we were at school, she would grab me and drag me off to talk just to her. She would ask a whole crowd of little fast questions.

"Does your mum cry?"

"Sometimes."

"If it was me, I'd cry bucketfuls every day."

I thought about Mum. "She's not really that kind of person," I said.

"Oh well."

And then, again, "Do you go and visit *the secret person*?"

"He's too far away."

"Do you miss him?"

"He's my dad."

I felt important when Lydia asked me things. Lydia could choose from so many people and she was picking me. I was just a bit worried that, as the days passed, I'd told her all the things I knew.

And I didn't really want to talk any more about Dad.

The other thing Lydia talked to me about was Molly Gardener.

"Everyone says Molly's dad disappeared. *Foof!*" Lydia popped her cheeks like a bag of crisps exploding and we both collapsed into laughs. "Like a puff of smoke. No more Dad. Like a genie coming out of a bottle, only the other way around. I bet you could find out what really happened to Molly's dad, Ella."

I stared at her, my heart hammering. I wondered if Lydia could hear it. No, I thought, I couldn't. Molly Gardener didn't talk to me. She didn't talk to anyone. Anyway, why was Lydia so interested in Molly's dad?

Lydia's face was all serious. "I love to know things. It's so exciting. And you've already found out more than anyone. We'll call it Operation 13... cos that's her house. You can be my Ella Criminella!"

What a horrible name. I didn't say anything while Lydia went on grinning at me... Maybe she would forget she'd thought of it.

Later that week, as I was walking out of school,

looking for Mum and Jack, I heard a voice calling my name and found Immy standing by the gates. "Do you live near here?" she asked.

"Yes," I said. "With my mum and my brother."

Immy grinned. "I've got a brother, Jacob. He's much older than me. He's at Mountview School. He's thirteen. We get the bus together."

"Oh," I said.

"Are you pleased with the shoes?"

"Oh yes," I said. "I love them. It was very kind of Lydia."

"Have you seen *Zombie Laundry*? It's hilarious!" Immy said. "I love stupid films. And adventures. Have you seen *Desert Whisper*? That is such a great film."

I shook my head.

"You *have* to see it."

I realised Mum was waving at me through the crowd.

"Well, see you tomorrow then," Immy called.

"Yes, see you."

As I walked away from her, I realised Immy never talked to me in that friendly way or came over to chat like that in school. It was odd. She had seemed really pleased to see me just now. In school she was often busy or dashing away. But, more than that, in school she seemed… different. Of course in school she was always with Lydia.

Yes, that was it; if Lydia was there, her friends always wanted to get her attention, to make her laugh. She was always at the centre, wasn't she?

✗

Every day, Mum seemed to be rushing. In the morning, she dashed to get our packed lunches and shouted at us to hurry up. There were lists everywhere and Mum kept saying we had to get ourselves organised. She said I had to pull my weight and look after Jack. "Don't make my life harder than it already is."

One Friday evening, when Jack and I had been at our new school for three weeks, Mum let a lady in and told us she would be looking after us after school each day. Mrs Reynolds looked like a grandma. She was wide with very white hair and a stick to lean on. She said, "Well, now, tell me about yourself," and I couldn't think of anything to say so I told her I was ten and she said, "Just the age where the brain really starts whirring. What's sixty-five plus seventy-three?"

"I hate maths," I said.

"I shall regard that as a challenge," she said.

She had a big bold booming voice and she could easily have told off an army, because when she spoke you had to listen. She leaned her stick against the kitchen top and started emptying the dishwasher.

"I'm so pleased this is all sorted out," Mum said.

Jack's bottom lip was out. "Where are you going?" he said to Mum.

"It's all right, Jack," Mum said, patting him. "I'll just be at work, sweetheart. That's why I've found Mrs Reynolds. And I need you both to be really helpful."

"Call me Sylvia," Mrs Reynolds said.

"Sylvia will be meeting you from school and making your tea, until I get back," Mum said.

"Will we still have baths?" Jack asked.

He's always asking silly questions. Sometimes he worries that Mum is going to go away and not come back because that's what happened with Dad. I don't worry about that.

Mum sighed. "Of course you'll still have baths. You'll still do all the usual things. It's just that Mrs Reynolds – I mean, Sylvia – will be here looking after you instead of me for a few hours."

Once Mrs Reynolds had gone and Jack was in bed, Mum came up to my room. She folded up the clothes on my chair then stood watching me taking photos of a squirrel on the tree outside my bedroom window. "Ella," she said, "you haven't told anyone about our family... about Dad, have you? It's just better if we keep things to ourselves."

I remembered Dad's face in the local paper, how Mum had cried and held on to me.

I stood there all still and stiff. How could I explain to Mum about Lydia? "I... I..."

Mum came up behind me now and put her arms round me so I could smell her fruit shampoo. I breathed in, staring hard at the tree, its jagged branches.

"This is our chance for a new start, sweetheart," Mum said, holding me. "I want it to be just us."

I nodded, turned and held out my phone to show her the photos I'd taken out of my window.

My mouth felt full of words, burning to come out. But I couldn't say any of them.

There was so much hope in Mum's voice.

Chapter 10
Shopping
Disaster

Dear Dad,

Do you remember when you and me and Jack went on the pedalo boats in Spain on that lake and your phone fell out of your pocket down into the water and you just laughed and said the fish would have to talk to your boss instead of you? It was so sunny and hot. Mum made me wear long sleeves and, when we were on the beach, she said I couldn't paddle because my feet were bad, and you said, well, you wouldn't paddle either, but then Jack filled a bucket in the sea and came back all the way with it and said, "Look, it's all right because I brought the sea to you."

Do you ever do a thing where you can't picture someone's face and you're really worried you won't recognise them? As long as I keep looking at the photo of all of us by my bed, I think I can sort of learn you. The best thing would be if you still had that red shirt. I don't know where your home clothes went. Do you still look the same? You haven't got a beard, have you?

Love, Ella

The next day was Saturday. Near teatime, Mum sent me to the small Co-op supermarket round the corner.

The doors swished open, and there was Molly Gardener right next to me in the fruit and veg aisle.

Molly's trolley was almost full. Our eyes met. Molly looked away.

I collected the yoghurts and milk Mum had asked me to get. At the till, Molly was in front of me. I waited, staring at her grubby grey tracksuit, the same one she had been wearing when Mum and I went to her house. Her black curly hair was tied back with a rubber band. She didn't turn. Could I ask some questions the way Lydia wanted me to? All the people in the queue would listen. What could I say? *Hello Molly, please tell me everything there is to know about you, right now!*

I chickened out.

She filled five carrier bags. She'd bought the whole shop!

Molly set off up the street before me. I could see her, head down, loaded up. But then, suddenly, lots of tins and packets fell out of her arms.

"Oh no!" she moaned. One of her bags must have split. She sank to her knees on the pavement, juggling shopping. A can rolled off the pile of bags and hit the pavement. An old lady dodged it as it rolled into the gutter.

I ran up. "I'll help you," I said, bending to grab a pack of yoghurts that was tangled up in the broken bag and pulling a loaf of bread from on top of the pile.

"Thanks," Molly murmured.

I went on transferring shopping into my bag and picking things up off the ground.

We both stood up. Now we had to walk back to Molly's house together. She didn't speak. I didn't either. "I'm actually helping you," I wanted to say. "Couldn't you just … talk to me?"

We went down her path. Now what? She wasn't exactly going to invite me inside, was she?

She unlocked the door.

"Here you are," I said, passing her the shopping in the doorway.

I turned to go. "I should get home. My mum's waiting."

"No!" Molly gulped a huge breath. "Stay and have some lemonade. Please?"

Molly Gardener was asking me in!

"If you just wait, I'll open the side gate," she said in a voice I hadn't heard before, pleading. "I'll only be a minute."

We locked eyes.

"OK," I said.

She closed the front door.

I texted Mum. **Met a school friend in our road. Back in twenty minutes.**

I stood, puzzled, staring at all the 'go away' stickers... and then went round to the side gate by the road and waited to be let in. Odd Molly Gardener. Why had she suddenly decided to be friendly?

Think how excited Lydia would be! I could imagine her, as if I had a mini Lydia on my shoulder, going, "Wahey. You're in! I told you, you were clever!"

✗

Molly's garden wasn't really a proper garden. It was just the back of a house and a square of tangled weeds and one tree. Then, at the end, there was a long shed. Two glasses of lemonade sat beside a coat laid on the long grass.

I waded over, weeds tickling my legs, pretending

this was normal.

"Sit down," Molly said.

I sat. Now I could hardly see for all the grass towering over me.

"Does my jumper fit you all right?" Molly gazed at the back door of her house, fingering the sides of her glass as if she was talking to the back door really.

Was someone in the kitchen? I craned to see through the windows but it just looked dark in there.

"Yeah." I sipped my lemonade. My glass didn't look very clean. It had greasy fingerprints. I looked down into the bubbles. "I'm sorry your shopping broke. They're not strong, those shop bags," I said.

Molly nodded.

Silence fell.

There wasn't anything to do in this garden. You couldn't play with a ball – you'd just lose it in the long grass.

"Just a minute." Molly got up, pushed her way down the garden and disappeared inside the shed at the end. She kept going off to places!

She came out of the shed carrying a brush and

what looked like a cat, but I realised it was the white rabbit. I stopped myself from saying, "Ooh, I've already met him." Close up, he was creamy white and fat with long limbs and a huge rabbit face with the floppiest long ears.

Molly held him up as if she'd won him. She smiled. I'd never seen her smile before. "This is Nelson." She sat down on the coat beside me, hauled him on to her knee and began brushing and murmuring to him.

"Oh, you are lucky," I said. Fur and eczema don't go together, Mum says. "I've never had a pet. My brother would love one. How much does he eat?"

"Oh, Nelson eats loads, don't you?" Molly kissed him on the nose. "There's a greengrocer on the main road – he saves the veg trimmings for me."

"How old is he?"

"Five."

"He's really big."

Molly definitely seemed much happier now Nelson was here.

"You're gorgeous, aren't you?" she told the rabbit, as if he might join in talking any minute.

But he just wiggled his nose.

Molly glanced at me. "Whenever I can't sleep, I come down and talk to him. I tell him everything."

I stared round the garden across the sea of stalks and shaggy heads. I'd never seen a garden with no proper plants and just a dead-looking tree in the middle. How odd – a house with too much in it and a garden with nothing.

Molly hadn't told me anything useful yet. "Are you...? Are there some more people in your family?" I asked.

Her mouth twitched. "No." She buried her face in Nelson's fur, murmuring, "He can hop really far."

"My brother is called Jack," I said, deciding to tell her about me instead. "He's six."

Molly looked up. "I'd like a brother." She pulled hairs out of the brush and brushed again. Nelson stretched himself across her legs.

"You can have him," I murmured, taking a long slurp of lemonade. "I love lemonade." That was true; I wasn't allowed it very often. "My mum's a computer programmer," I told her. "That's why we moved; cos Mum got a new job."

Molly looked away. "I haven't got a computer,"

she said in a fierce sort of voice. "I have to use the ones at school."

We both slurped lemonade again.

Molly got up. "Come and see Nelson's cage."

I blinked in the gloomy shed, trying to look interested in her rabbit hutch, breathing in the sweet rabbity smell. I stared at Nelson's water bottle and the bags of rabbit food and bedding. There wasn't anything else to see. "Nelson's allowed anywhere but he usually sleeps in here," Molly said.

When we came out into the sunshine again, Molly slid down between the shed and the fence and grabbed a fistful of leaves. "Dandelions," she said. "His favourite."

Then, sudden and loud from the house came "Mols!", then louder, "Mols?" That woman's voice calling. Just like last time.

Chapter 11
Ella Criminella

Dear Dad,

Last night I dreamed you came home, just for an evening, because the prison was closed – maybe it was a holiday. All the prisoners came rushing out and you were all holding a special cake for your families and you rushed up to me and hugged me. Then you disappeared.

You were in a bright green jacket.

Ella

Molly looked terrified. She bundled the huge rabbit into my arms and stuffed the leaves in my hands. "Take care of him," she said, rushing away. The kitchen door clunked shut.

Nelson was really heavy – heavier than the shopping, and solid, with clambering legs that dug in. My hands seemed to prickle. What if I was allergic?

Why had Molly made me hold him anyway? Couldn't I just let him hop around? He seemed too fat to run fast. I eased him down on to the coat beside me with his leaves and clicked three pictures on my phone, sending them straight to Lydia. I texted, **Operation 13. Here's Molly's rabbit eating.**

Nelson's machine-like jaws polished off the leaves so quickly. He stretched and seemed to gather his back legs into himself. Maybe, sometimes, with the grass so long, he got lost and Molly had to use a fishing net to find him. I picked him up again and wandered a little way towards the kitchen. It was a greenish kind of dark inside. The paint was peeling off the window. I walked back down the garden and took Nelson to see the fence. He must have seen it before.

Rabbits don't say anything – he can't have been very impressed.

How long was Molly going to be? I looked back at the house. There was a feeling of secrets at Molly's.

I sat down on the coat again in a sort of rabbit-bundling way, managing not to drop Nelson. He lolled there on my knee, all warm, a great big body, sniffing at the grass around us. I began to like the feeling, the vibration of him.

Molly came out from the back door again and sat down. "Sorry," she said.

"Did someone call you?" I asked softly.

Molly made a tiny sound. "Mmm." Her whole body sagged, as if someone had unpacked all her stuffing. Her eyes flicked back to the house. She scooped Nelson off my knees. All in a rush she said, "Mum's busy. She... um... collects furniture." Her face had that fierce look again, as if she was saying don't ask me about this. She hugged Nelson to her. "Don't go in my house," she said. "Don't *ever* go in my house."

Her words felt like a slap – furious.

She still didn't look at me, just stroked Nelson's ears over and over.

That's how you lie. It's very hard to lie and look into a person's eyes. That's why teachers make you look at them.

There had to be something really scary inside Molly's house. "No, no, I won't," I said.

She looked like she might cry. Why was her face so sad? Why had she spoken to me like that? I couldn't tell her that I'd already been inside her house. "Molly, I—" I began.

But my phone beeped. I checked it. A message from Lydia. **Clever old Ella Criminella! Can't wait to hear all the goss.**

"I have to go now," I said. "Mum's invited someone."

✗

On Monday, at lunchtime, Lydia beckoned me over to sit on the field with Rachel, Sophie and Immy. They were discussing the teachers' first names. The others seemed to know nearly all of them. "Mr Goldman is Charlie and Miss Evans is Helen. She looks like a Helen," Sophie said.

"What about Mr Gibbons?" Rachel asked. "No one's found out his."

"Plonkybrain," Immy suggested.

"Stop it, Immy. This is serious," Lydia said.

"No it isn't," Immy said.

Lydia's face was concentrating. "OK then, does anyone know Miss Stevenson's? I think she's an Amy. You can sometimes find out teachers' names if you just listen when they talk to other teachers and pretend you're not really there. The drinking fountain's a good place. Or carrying things by the office."

"I know when Mr Hales's birthday is – 29th May!" Immy said.

Lydia scrunched up her eyes against the sun. "I knew that anyway." She shielded her eyes with her hand, gazing at Immy. "If your eyebrows meet in the middle, does that mean you're turning into a wolf?"

Immy's fingers flew to the space above her nose.

Everyone giggled. I joined in. I didn't think Immy looked odd at all but everyone else was laughing.

Immy sprang up. "You're not funny." Her mouth was wobbling like Jack's does sometimes. "My mum says people have different amounts of hair. It's just normal."

Lydia stretched her legs out. She let out a little

growl.

"Stop it," Immy said.

Lydia growled louder.

Immy walked away, rubbing her eyes with the back of her hand.

"Ella and me are going to talk *alone now*," Lydia told the others.

"All right," Sophie said crossly, "be like that." She got up and strutted away arm in arm with Rachel.

Lydia pulled me closer. "Back to Operation 13." She locked her arm into mine. "I need my Ella Criminella."

I felt a kind of jolt, hearing that name again. "I don't like that name. It's horrible."

But Lydia poked me, hard. "It's a joke. It's funny." She pointed to Molly bent over her notebook on the wall. "First things first: Molly's dad?"

"I still don't know about him," I said, feeling odd about that question. "She said there was just her and her mum." I remembered the fierce way Molly had told me.

"Didn't you see any other people at her house?"

I felt as if I was a witness in a trial. "I didn't go inside this time," I said. "We sat in her garden.

But she said her mum is a furniture collector."

"Couldn't you have gone in to the loo?"

"She didn't want me to. She's got a rabbit. She really loves it, kissing it like *mwah, mwah*. I had to look after it when someone called."

"And that was when you sent me the photo…? Mmm, could be anyone's rabbit."

"But we know it's hers."

"It's still not very interesting. Loads of people have rabbits." Lydia sighed. "Tell me about the first time you went inside."

"Well…" I pictured the dark room, the hand stretching out to me. I shuddered. "I saw a person… a long trailing sort of dark cloak… a really long white hand…"

"This is so creepy!" Lydia murmured, squeezing my arm. "Hey, Ella, I know what… Molly's dad got turned into a rabbit. He's under a spell!"

I laughed. Lydia pretended to have rabbit ears, waggling her hands above her head. "That's it! You said she kissed her rabbit all the time. Maybe she's trying to get her dad back. It's like the frog prince only… with rabbits!" She did her little high trilling laugh, like music. "That's it. My clever Ella Criminella. Her mum makes her dad disappear …

and those piles of things in the house... they are... the enchanted palace. It's like Rapunzel in the tower. Or Sleeping Beauty." Lydia's face switched suddenly to serious and fixed. "Go and sit with Molly when we go back in this afternoon."

I didn't know what to say. "But no one sits next to her."

"She'll let you," Lydia said. "She must like you. She invited you. You have to do this, Ella."

Chapter 12
Investigating

Dear Dad,

The art room at Moor Lane is full of things to draw. There's a skeleton in a bowler hat. Miss Denby showed us how to make photos with mixtures of things called still lifes. If I go to a place and take a photo I just select, zoom, click. Maybe I could work for a newspaper.

Hope your food is getting better. Jack hid some broccoli in a plant. I've been looking after your crocodile key ring with the big wide mouth. Do you remember when I gave it to you for your birthday?

Here is a photo of a squirrel on the tree outside my bedroom window, a pet rabbit and one of Jack making his cold custard face. Isn't the rabbit fat? He's called Nelson.

Love, Ella

I joined the line-up and, when I got back into Willow class, I went to the back of the classroom where Molly had already sat down. I stood there holding my bag. Molly looked slowly up at me, piled up her things and made space for me.

"Thanks," I said and sat down.

Oh wow – it worked! I waited a bit and then grinned over at Lydia, but I couldn't catch her eye. She was giggling with Sophie. Being Lydia's friend sometimes felt like a thin thing, a thing that might melt away and, just for a horrid moment, I felt as if they might be giggling about me. But then I thought, no, Lydia's just excited. I still wished she'd look at me, though.

Molly did talk to me a little bit, but with comments like, "Have you finished?" or "Can I turn it over now?" When we shared a worksheet I showed her one of my answers to a question about owl pellets. She worked so quietly she could almost not have been there. I didn't feel as if me being next to her mattered. Maybe she was thinking about something else when she was in school. There was a smell around Molly too: old clothes. I wished I was next to Lydia and laughing.

It couldn't hurt Molly though, could it – me

finding things out?

That afternoon, Mrs Reynolds collected Jack first, because he got out five minutes before me from the other playground. She and Jack were waiting when Mr Hales let us out. Mrs Reynolds waved.

"Is that your grandma?" Lydia asked, appearing beside me.

"No. She's a childminder," I said, then added quickly, "for Jack."

Mrs Reynolds went on sitting in the sunshine with her stick next to her and Jack leaping behind her along the planter while all the other mums and dads stood and talked to each other. I had to point her out to Mr Hales so he would let her collect me.

"Why is she so old?" Lydia asked.

I shrugged. "She just is."

"We mustn't forget about Operation 13," Lydia said. "Sit with Molly tomorrow."

"But I…"

"Gotta dash, Criminella," Lydia said. "Write it down. Like a proper investigator. I need to find Immy."

✗

I wished Mrs Reynolds only collected Jack. Nearly everyone in my class was allowed to walk home on their own or with a friend. I rushed into the office to collect my phone, and that made me feel better because I could play on it all the way home, until Mrs Reynolds said, "Put that away now, Ella, unless you have an actual call to make."

I gaped at her. I hadn't had my phone all day and now she was stopping me having it for no reason.

Mrs Reynolds' face had very papery skin. She tucked her stick under her arm and reached out to take my hand. I pulled away. Did she think I was a baby? Jack flung her arm around on the other side and she wobbled and nearly fell over. "All right then, let's agree that you both walk sensibly beside me," she said, starting to lean on the stick again. "How was your day?"

We walked home very slowly. At home, she made us wash our hands and then we had juice and biscuits. She wasn't that bad, just kept asking me things, especially maths things. She made us do homework. Jack read her his reading book and I filled in two sheets. Then Mrs Reynolds checked them as if she was the teacher.

I was getting sick of having to be good. I would have done all the maths questions in the world soon. Then Mrs Reynolds suddenly said, "Telly on." She switched on a quiz. The contestants were being asked about geography and books and European football clubs and Mrs Reynolds started shouting out the answers from the kitchen while she made pasta sauce.

I wondered if Mum had told Mrs Reynolds about Dad. He loves quizzes.

Jack and I were allowed upstairs now. I could still hear Mrs Reynolds shouting answers, as if she was one of the contestants in the TV studio too. Jack called me a slug and I slammed my bedroom door so he couldn't come in, and sat on my bed. I made a list of things I already knew about Molly and I pinned it up, like a police chief.

Molly Gardener is very tall.

She lives at number 13 Ash Grove.

She goes to Moor Lane School.

She is in Willow class.

She has a rabbit called Nelson.

Her back garden is a mess.

Her house is full of old furniture and odd things in the wrong places.

Someone is in the house. They are wearing a long black coat and they have a long white hand.

Molly shops at the Co-op.

She always has a notebook with her.

She seems scared.

She often wears trainers but the teachers don't tell her off. Why?

She hardly ever gives her homework in but Mr Hales doesn't get cross. Why?

Lydia thinks her mum is a witch and she turned her dad into a rabbit.

Chapter 13
Something
Strange

Dad

I've been thinking about the view out of your window. I would not like to only see a wire fence. From my classroom, we can see playing fields and a line of back gardens and from home I can see our new garden and the tree.

I would never throw things out of my window. That sounds bad. You don't do it, do you? If a person is in prison and they do a bad thing, do they get punished? I know you said you don't like hearing keys jingling, but maybe when you come home, you might change your mind.

It's raining today – great big fat drops. I got wet coming home. Do prisoners have raincoats with hoods or umbrellas? Can you jump in the puddles? If you all jumped at once, would it make a big wave?

Mum is very busy at work. She even works in bed!!

I am sorry you can't have your own phone. Could you borrow one really quickly and text me a picture of you with your friends? Someone must have one. Even Mrs Reynolds has one and she is old and doesn't like it much. I showed her how to change the ringtone. She's got a jungle one now and she laughs every time it rings but that doesn't happen very often.

Here is a photo of Mum and me and Jack that Mrs Reynolds took.

Love, Ella

I didn't want to sit with Molly but I did it all the rest of that week.

She didn't seem to care either way. She seemed gloomy, busy in her head. And she dashed away to her notebook half the time. There wasn't much to report.

Molly sighed a lot. She was a miserable kind of person, I decided.

I made careful notes for Lydia.

1. Molly's lunch – Molly has some bread and cheese and an apple for lunch.
2. Pencils – she doesn't even have her own colouring pencils.
3. She never puts her hand up.
4. Notebook, of course. She has that out a lot, at break and lunchtime. It is a little woven gold one with a cord wrapped round it and white pages.

"Did you look inside it?" Lydia asked.

"No," I said. "I've never had a chance. Molly's always there."

5. Bank card. Molly also has a red bank card in her rucksack. I saw it when she was putting her lunchbox back.

I made sure Lydia knew that. "She does have

money," I said.

"How much?"

"She has a bank card – for getting money out."

I could tell I had impressed her.

"Really? Do you think she's really rich then?" Lydia asked.

"She doesn't look as if she's got loads of money."

Lydia's eyes were shining. "Wish I had a bank card. I'd spend a million, million pounds before Mum and Dad even noticed the card was gone."

I was sure Lydia was pleased with me now. She must be. But she was frowning. "Operation 13's not very interesting yet, is it?" she said. "Get Molly to invite you again."

"She might not."

"Oh, Ella, interview people then. If you found out something interesting, I'd ask Mum if you can come to my house for tea."

For tea! My stomach felt squirmy. That would only be if I found out more.

Lydia pouted. "I thought you would have found out something really exciting by now. It's not like Molly's a master criminal or something." She giggled. "I expect *you* know a lot more about *that kind of thing!"*

I stared at her. *Master criminal... That kind of thing...*

But then Lydia squeezed my arm and tickled me. "Only joking!" she called.

"Must dash. I'm going round to Rachel's."

I had a sudden pang of aloneness. I wished Grace was with me again and I could go round to her house the way I used to. Grace who understood. Grace who was kind.

Hurt feelings still flooded me even after Lydia danced away to get her bag. Did she think I knew lots of criminals? Was that why she'd made up that name for me?

All the rest of the day, sitting beside grumpy Molly Gardener, I worried about whether Lydia would tell anyone else the truth about my dad, if she thought it was funny or didn't matter. I studied the other girls from the sleepover... Hannah, Rachel, Sophie, Immy, Zing. I watched them tell stories and chat, standing quietly near them. Did they think I was a criminal sort of person? None of them spoke to me very much. Was that because they didn't think I was a nice person?

I'd find out more about Molly. That was what

Lydia had asked me to do.

✗

I volunteered to pick up extra shopping we needed at the Co-op. Mrs Reynolds gave me the money and a bag and said, "That's the sort of girl I want to see."

I stood with my shopping at the till and decided to ask the Co-op lady some questions. "Do you know Molly Gardener?" I asked.

"I know everyone, love. I've known the Gardeners for years, as it happens. Are you buying that broccoli?"

"Oh, yes please." I opened my shopping bag and she began scanning things. I saw she had a badge on her uniform saying "MY NAME'S GEMMA. I'M HERE TO HELP". That made me feel better.

"It's just we need to speak to her mum or dad about some furniture… My mum wants to buy some." I clutched my money, rolling the coins around between my fingers.

"Sorry, can't help you there. You'd have to ask her."

"Well, we're new and I … well, nobody answered the door." I could feel my face getting red.

"Maybe they don't want any callers then." Gemma eyed me sharply.

Lydia would think I hadn't tried hard enough. I could imagine her piercing stare. "But you *must* know if Molly's mum does her shopping here..." I said.

The lady frowned. She opened her mouth, then she seemed to decide not to say something and shut it, hard.

"I mean, I just wondered if it was Molly's mum who put the advert in your window... about the school uniform. I bought her jumper," I said.

Gemma's face became the telling-off face grown-ups use. "Some people ask too many questions," she said. "Now, off you go. I've people to serve."

Her voice echoed as I walked away. I rushed home with the shopping and a great big smile on my face. A thrill kept running through me. There was definitely a mystery.

Lydia was bound to invite me back to her house now!

Chapter 14
You're a
Photographer

Hi Dad,

I don't have the swingball set – I think it got broken when we moved. I would like a trampoline but Mum says it would fill the whole garden, so forget it, sunshine. But I haven't. I think you would like a trampoline too, Dad.

Jack can tie his tie now. He's not very good at it though. Their teachers help them take them off, otherwise the whole PE lesson gets wasted. He's got lots of friends. Why do you keep asking about Jack? He's not even bothering to write to you.

Love Ella

Lydia had lots of ideas at the next art club, when I told her about the lady from the Co-op and the warning.

"Maybe Molly's parents had a battle and her mum shot her dad with an old-fashioned gun," she whispered, choosing a green pencil and drawing a hard line across her paper. "Maybe she buried the dad under the floor and they collected all that furniture to put on top... or, Ella, maybe she keeps him prisoner behind the fireplace and feeds him only at weekends... or..."

I got tired of listening. I found myself only answering some of Lydia's questions, or just nodding. I wanted to think about my picture. The sea cave was taking shape.

The room became quieter, except for people humming to the radio.

"Great work, Ella," said Miss Denby the next time she passed. "It's odd how it's always more beautiful if you rip the paper. Have you done this kind of collage before?"

"No," I said. "But I like it."

After half an hour, Lydia had begun to really annoy me. Her voice got harder to ignore. And she was complaining again.

"Why won't Miss Denby come and help me?" she whinged.

She's been over about ten times already, I thought. *You wave your hand around so much you're like a scarecrow in a high wind.*

"Yours is really good," Lydia said, poking my sea picture, lifting up the glued edges at one side. "That place there needs more bits though. Do you want me to stick some more on?"

"No," I said. I held my hand over it.

"Do you want to borrow my brush pen?" Lydia asked next.

"No, thanks, it's fine."

"Miss! Mine's rubbish," Lydia shouted. "I'm stuck!"

Lydia's picture was OK but she never sat and thought, just splashed paint. She reminded me of Jack doing art: all accidents and mess.

"I'm helping Hassan," called Miss Denby from the other side of the art room. "You've only just started, Lydia. See if you can solve the problem on your own."

At the end of the club, everyone propped their work up and Miss Denby talked about what they were each working on.

"Very expressive, Lydia," she said.

Lydia scowled.

Miss Denby moved on to mine. "Ella took this photo herself. See how the dark cave interior frames the photo. Great composition, Ella. You're a photographer. Photos can sometimes get right inside the heart of a thing. When you've finished the collage, how about creating some more of your interesting photos?"

I loved the idea. I was so lit up about it I told Mum at bedtime.

"Miss Denby, my art teacher, wants me to do more photography."

"That's great, love," said Mum. "I'm glad you're loving the phone. We must tell Grandma."

I started to look out for more things to photograph. I loved little details, like the speckles on a bunch of bananas. Maybe my camera could help with Operation 13. Photos could give me clues.

I would investigate more now I was a photographer.

✗

Every evening, Mrs Reynolds began watching her quiz at five o'clock. From "Welcome to your host" until the news, Jack and I were allowed to play in our rooms. She didn't call us down to wash our hands for tea for a whole 45 minutes. So, I waited till the quiz started, then nipped out of the front door instead of going upstairs.

First, I looked for lights on in the windows at number 13. With my nose squashed up against a hole in the fence, I could see a light on, even though it wasn't dark yet. I saw shapes in there. I could even make out voices. If I fitted my phone in a knothole in the fence, I could take a picture of the kitchen window.

I observed Molly's house on Tuesday and Wednesday. I filled in my notebook. Kitchen light on 5.20 p.m. Voices. Back door shut. Nelson in garden.

Kitchen light on 5.20 p.m. Voices. Radio. Back door shut.

Not very interesting.

✗

On Thursday evening, I heard someone behind me when I had just put my phone up to the hole in the fence. I swung round to find Jack looking thrilled with himself. "What are you doing, Ella?"

"Go away."

"No, not till you tell me what you're doing."

'I'm a detective. A spy," I said.

His little face lit up.

"I can take pictures. Put together clues," I told him.

"Why?"

"Because I want to find out… things."

I showed him how I could take a picture through the fence. "You have to be older to have a phone to investigate like this. You're not mature enough," I told him.

"Well, I am mature," he said. "And spies don't use phones; they use magnifying glasses and they dust for fingerprints."

"How do you know?"

"I just do." His mouth wobbled. "Oh, Ella, you'll get in trouble."

"No I won't. You can stay if you're quiet."

Jack put his finger to his lips.

As Jack and I stared, a dark flapping shape appeared in the kitchen. The long trailing arms made it look like a strange shadow puppet floating in the air.

"What's that?" Jack squeaked.

"I don't know. I can't see properly." I held my

phone in the gap. *Click.*

"I don't like it here, Ella," Jack whispered. "What if it comes out and gets us?"

I pushed him away. "I told you, you weren't mature enough. Just go home."

The dark shape had gone out of view now.

A sound began inside the house: a rasping choking sort of cough.

"You have to come too!" Jack's voice rose to a wail. He clutched my arm.

"Jack, you're a pain!" I said, steering him back towards home. "You're *not* coming again."

I checked the photo when I got in. "Is it a witch?" Jack whispered. "Or is it Batman?"

"It's too blurry," I said.

You could see the person shape, the long floating arms. Maybe Lydia would be pleased with that. She might.

Here is the Creature from the Black Lagoon, I texted, sending her the photo.

✗

I lay in the dark later, thinking about Molly's house and listening to the clicking of Mum working on her computer downstairs.

Even though I liked making up the story with

Lydia, I hadn't liked hearing the coughing. People don't cough in fairy tales.

I dreamed about the inside of number 13 but it had grown into a huge maze: eerie shapes and towers, trees and the white rabbit hopping, always a little way in front – that bobbing white tail just disappearing out of view, leading me always to the figure in black with the trailing arms. Trapping me.

Chapter 15
A Notebook
Leads to
Trouble

Dad,

I wasn't rude about it and I didn't argue with Mum. I don't care about stupid trampolines. It's just why does Mum say "We'll see" when she really means "no" because it makes Jack think she might be going to say yes?

I like Mum's chopped-off haircut too. She says she is still getting used to it.

I didn't know Grandma came to visit you. She rings Mum sometimes but Mum always hangs up.

I took a close-up photo of some swans on the river. Do you like it? Swans' necks are so long!

Did I tell you that my uniform is green? I think orange is my favourite colour now. Why don't people have orange cars? We would never lose our car in a car park like we did in Edinburgh. Or, maybe, we could have stripy or spotty cars. I would choose an orange one with purple stripes. Maybe it's too difficult to draw the straight lines for the stripes.

Jack says he hasn't forgotten you – you don't need to worry about that.

Ella

As half-term got nearer, we had an activities day at school with lots of sports. The teachers made us hold up the sides of a huge coloured parachute and run underneath so it made a cave. We all cheered and ran races. One game was to see how far you could throw a welly and Stiggy's throw went spinning wide and high and hit Mr Ponting, the caretaker, but he just grinned and threw it back.

I sat on a bench with Lydia and her group while the races were happening, waiting for our class to be called. Molly Gardener was sitting on her own, writing in her notebook.

Mr Hales called us all for the hurdles. I'm not very fast at running so I didn't get chosen for the finals. But Molly did. As she was about to run, she pressed her notebook into my hands. "Please, look after this." She stood quietly on the line then took off, dashing over the hurdles, her legs dipping and flying.

Lydia grabbed the notebook. She unwound the lace. I looked too. Pictures, sketches. A lot were of Nelson: Nelson hopping, Nelson eating, his nose, his face. "Well, that's useless," Lydia said, thrusting the book back into my hands. "I thought it was a diary. She hasn't written anything." She skipped away.

The next race was just ending. Zamir flew so fast across the finishing line that he couldn't stop and he ploughed into a table of teachers keeping score. Everyone was laughing.

I watched Molly run. I wished I could take a photo, catch the moment when she flew, the high point of each jump. I looked again at her notebook, further on, towards the back. These sketches weren't like anything I'd ever seen. They were shadowy, like shapes and faces rising out of smoke: crying eyes, hands, strange objects. I lingered over some of the dark smudgy faces. They seemed to be calling out to me.

Molly appeared beside me, panting from the race.

"I was just looking," I said, handing her notebook back. "Your drawings are really good."

Molly flushed, wrapped the lace round it over and over.

"You should come to art club," I said.

✗

Next time I went to art club I met Molly at the door. I must have looked surprised but she just did a sort of nod towards me and we both went inside.

She must have already checked with Miss Denby because Miss Denby looked up from a pile of prints she was sorting and smiled at both of us. "Molly tells me you encouraged her to come, Ella. I'm so glad."

"Oh, yes," I said, "I did."

"Why don't you both sit together since you know each other?" Miss Denby said.

Molly collected a pot of charcoal pencils and white paper and began drawing immediately.

I was keen to get started too. I flicked through the pictures on my phone and found some I had taken by the river when Jack and I went to feed the ducks.

"Can I have a look?" Miss Denby asked.

I showed her.

"I really think photography could be your thing," she said. "Would you like to try making some bigger compositions?" She went to her desk and brought out the school digital camera. "You'll have to learn its features, but you seem to have a real eye for this."

"Oh wow," I said, "can I?"

"This is how you zoom... Flash is here. Think of a camera as an eye on the world." She gathered up things for me to photograph. "How about this tiny stuffed alligator... these opera glasses...?"

The art room filled with other people from the club but I was far away... in a new land, the radio playing, trying out new positions for the objects, experimenting with their shadows...

The door slammed.

I looked up.

Lydia with her art case.

There was no space next to me now Molly was sitting beside me.

Lydia's mouth froze in a hard pout. "Where am I supposed to sit?" she demanded.

"There are lots of places to sit, Lydia. You are late. Why don't you choose one over there?" Miss Denby pointed to the tables on the other side of the room. "I've put Molly next to Ella because they know each other. But you know everyone, don't you?"

Lydia's face curled into the scariest snarl. I gulped and put down the camera.

Was she cross because I was sitting with Molly? That didn't make sense. She was always wanting me to sit with Molly. She huffed and plonked herself down one table away and slowly began to unpack, glaring at me. I stood there in a panicky kind of blur.

"Miss Denby," she moaned, "I'm still waiting for some help and this picture is rubbish." Then, a few minutes later: "Miss, someone's taken my green ink and Mum'll have to ring the school!"

I tried to think about the little alligator… the way its stiff body made shadows on the pale grey table… but my heart was hammering and the camera kept wobbling.

Lydia got up and prowled around. She stopped behind Molly. "Oooh, is that your rabbit you're drawing?"

Molly's head came slowly up. Her eyes looked like a person who's heard a very distant noise. She seemed to think for a moment, then she looked down at her paper and began to draw again.

Lydia stiffened. "I asked you a question," she said loud and crisp and clear. "What's wrong with you?"

Molly's head stayed down.

"Everyone talks in clubs," Lydia snapped.

It was like being in a storm and trying to keep

from getting soaked. Or washed away. But I still couldn't understand. Why was Lydia *so* angry?

"Why are you wandering about, Lydia?" Miss Denby called.

"I needed more paper."

"Well, get some then and go back to your seat."

Being ignored by Molly seemed to make Lydia more furious than anything else could have. She flounced away and sat down, sighing loudly. "I've got too many pens, miss. I can't decide what to start with. Everything's ruined!"

A few moments later, I went to the sink to wash my hands and Lydia shot over beside me. "Why is *she* here?" she hissed.

"I ... I ... Molly's really good at art," I whispered. "I thought you'd be pleased."

"She is *not* good at art." Lydia looked as if she was going to explode. "*She is rubbish at art!*"

My heart hammered. "S-s-sorry," I said. "Do you want me to sit next to you?"

"It's too late. I don't care where you sit!"

I scrubbed at my wrist under the water. "I'm really sorry. I just saw Molly's notebook at the sports day and I thought her drawings were...

em… really good."

"Well, then you are stupid, Ella Mackay!" Lydia flounced away and sat down again.

I walked slowly back. Molly was still carrying on with her soft careful sketching without looking up.

What was Lydia going to do?

Chapter 16
Watermelon
Girl

Dear Dad,

Are you all right?

The bad thing you did – the stealing – why did you do that, Dad? Where has the money gone? Did you buy something? I could take it back. If you say sorry and promise never to do that again, will they let you come home? When Jack took the mini octopus, you made him say sorry and the shopkeeper put it back on the shelf. I don't want us to have extra money. I could stop having sweets (not chocolate) and if I told Jack he would stop too – that would make a lot of money. I'll ask Mrs Reynolds to do it in a sum and pretend it's for school. Could we save up? How much?

Love, Ella

Next day, in Willow class, I sat with Molly and Bryony as usual and, after the maths test, when I read out the wrong answer, there was a little ripple of laughs from where Lydia sat. I felt myself go scarlet. They were talking about me.

The clenching feeling began in my stomach.

Did Lydia's friends know about Dad now?

I peeped over. Zing did a little shrug and turned away from me. Sophie whispered something to Rachel.

Sophie was definitely the first one Lydia would choose. She'd take her in a corner, maybe invite her for tea. Yes, that's how it would be. "Do you want to know something really juicy about Ella... Well...?"

Each time I looked over, Lydia's eyes fixed on me, concentrating, unblinking, like a cat on a fence when you try to win the staring match and you never do.

I went into the loos and Sophie came out, saw me, made her face blank and walked past.

Rachel pushed a tiny slip of paper into my school planner saying, "I'm not taking sides, but I'm going to have to hate you. Love Rachel."

On the Internet, Jack and I once watched

a watermelon being exploded. It was shown so slowly you could see the moment when the sides split and the whole shape of the melon was opening and breaking, before all the chunks and juice flew up in a hail of pink gunk. That was me. Lydia had exploded me and all the little pieces were trying to be Ella shape but there was no shape any more, just flying bits.

Had Lydia told them all? Even if she hadn't, she could, any time she wanted. My secret would spread right round school until the teachers were looking at me too, thinking I was a bad person when they hardly even knew me. No one would ever invite me to anything.

I answered when people spoke to me, ate my lunch. I even did some colouring with Bryony. But I wasn't a proper whole person.

And how could I go back to art club again after half-term? Maybe I should just not go. Or ask Molly to stop going? Would Molly leave the club if I asked her? What did Lydia want me to do? How could I make her like me again?

At home, Jack was being a pain. I discovered a mouldy apple in my bed so I wedged a chair under the door handle of his room. "You're trapped," I told him. "I will never let you out. You will starve to death and no one will ever find you!" He twisted the door handle and hammered on the door but it held firm. He howled so loudly that Mrs Reynolds came and found us and made us sit on opposite sides of the kitchen and stare at each other until Mum got home. Mum was furious. She made me say sorry and threatened to take my phone away.

We broke up for half-term. A whole week with no one to play with except stupid Jack and Mrs Reynolds looking after us so Mum could be at work.

Mrs Reynolds put a plastic tunnel in the garden for Jack but then we fought because we both tried to get inside at the exact same moment and the side got torn. Mrs Reynolds said we should learn a lesson from that. Then Jack had his friend Sammy round and they ran up and down the garden screaming and throwing each other into the wet leaves and I just stayed in my room and said no thanks when Mrs Reynolds asked me if I'd like to make fairy cakes and decorate them. She let me wander by the river while she and Jack fed the ducks and I took lots of photos. I tried texting Grace again but she didn't reply.

✗

I listened to the noise of my class on the first day back, so full of people calling out to their friends. I nodded to Molly and sat beside her and Bryony. I didn't look at Lydia's group, even though I could hear them giggling and chatting. I wanted them to forget me. I would fade and fade and be… nobody.

But, at break, Lydia came to find me. "Ella," she said. "Come outside."

We put our coats on and walked out into the school garden. Everything was dead out there. I blew on my hands and saw my breath spiralling up. I waited for Lydia to say something.

She raked her shoe along the edge of the gravel. "I've forgiven you," she said in a firm voice.

"Have you?" I asked.

We walked up and down and watched some infants watering the dead plants.

"Yes. But I want Operation 13 to be solved. The picture you sent me is too blurry. You're a photographer, Miss Denby said."

My stomach started to grip me again. "I don't understand."

"I want a picture of the strange dark creature, a proper photo, right in the room."

Lydia had planned what she was going to say.

"I know you can do it. You've been my brave Ella Criminella and you're nearly finished. When this is all over, we'll know the truth."

"But… it's Molly's house," I said.

"I know. Find an excuse. You'll think of one."

"But…"

"I don't want to tell all the others about your dad being a criminal but… I might have to… if you forget to help me."

I stared into Lydia's cold blue eyes. "Prove to me how brave you are," she said. "Then we'll forget everything. Everything. Start again with a new Ella."

I had to sit next to Molly the rest of that day. The sneaking thing Lydia had told me to do seemed to be in the air all around me.

I would be a burglar.

Miss Denby told me, in art club, that Aborigines in Australia believe that when you take a photo you are stealing a part of someone's soul. My stomach rolled and coiled. I flicked a look at Molly working quietly beside me. She seemed to feel my eyes and looked up. I wished I could tell her all of a sudden. Would she understand? No, of course she wouldn't. I looked down at my paper again and heard her sigh.

Don't ever *go in my house*, she'd said.

I would tell Lydia no.

I rubbed my wrist with my pen lid: back, forward, back, forward.

Lydia had said we could start again with a new Ella. If she did forget about Dad, people in my class might like me. Moor Lane might be home. I might get invited to someone's house for tea. Tears started in my eyes. Lydia hadn't said anything about coming for tea, had she? She was making me go in Molly's house and take the photo, but it wasn't fun.

Had Dad felt like this about the money stealing? He must have, mustn't he? Did he go and get the money on a dark night, like burglars in stories? Did he carry it in a big dark bag... creeping, sneaking...?

My whole body turned hot. I *would* take that

photo. Tonight.

I realised suddenly that lots of my class were staring at me. I must have been scraping at my hand with the pen lid. A jagged 'V' of skin had started to bleed. I licked the sore place, pulled my jumper over it.

"Are you all right, Ella?" Mr Hales asked.

"Y-y-yes. I just can't do number six." My head went down to stare at my page again.

"We'll go over them in a minute," Mr Hales said.

Chapter 17
Surprise!

Dad,

Have you got some friends in prison? Please could you tell me their names?

I'm wondering if we could come and see you when it's Christmas. I think we should come. If we're staying at Grandma's, we will be near you – I looked on a map. Or, could you have a holiday from being in prison, just for a weekend or something?

Love, Ella

A long evening with Mrs Reynolds fussing over our homework while I waited for the dark.

At half past nine, after Mum had come up to say goodnight, she went back down and started typing. I pulled on all my clothes and put my coat on top, collected what I needed, softly closed the front door and stepped out into the cold night air. Street lamps made pools of light. There was nobody about. A car drove by, its bright headlights sweeping on and down and away.

What would I see inside the darkness of the maze? I remembered the camera in the art room, the feeling of the camera's eye looking... choosing. Like a fox on a dark night hunting for food. It wouldn't be me taking a picture – it would be a camera eye catching the truth. Yes, that felt better.

I held my phone in my hand. The bulky weight in my pocket: the green and yellow stripy notebook rubbed against my leg. It was one from our family holiday two years ago, before Dad was taken away. He had been with me when I chose it, tapping impatiently on his phone, trying to get a signal in the little Spanish shop full of hats and bags and souvenirs, saying, "Does it really matter so much which one, Ella?" Then laughing when I said, "Yes, Dad, it really does."

Don't think. All ready to start again with a new Ella.

If I went in fast, even the creature person wouldn't really see me. Lydia was only asking for a *click* – less than a second. Like a blink. I would pretend I'd forgotten that Molly had told me not to go inside her house. I would say, "Oh, whoops, sorry about that. I'm just off anyway. No harm done."

Mum would never know I'd told Lydia about Dad.

No harm done.

I turned into the lane of garages, pulled myself up over the fence, scraping my legs on the dry wood and fell. Ow! I slid between Nelson's cage and Molly's fence and pushed through the long grass. Nelson must be listening to me.

There was no light on in the kitchen. The back door wasn't locked.

The kitchen smelled sour, like an old cloth. There were jars and packets on the surfaces. I opened the door into the hall. A hush, like a library. My legs felt all wobbly. Here it was again:

the feeling of all the piled-up things closing round me. A wardrobe blocked my way. I stepped round, crashed against a chimney pot. A web trailed across my mouth. Yuck. I switched on the torch on my phone. I gazed around, trembling beside some huge piece of furniture with carved figures on it – faces with wide grins... snakeish – leaping...

I spun round. A rocking horse wobbled above me, its bright glaring mouth ready to swallow me. My heart did a dance of terror. The spectre of Molly's mum would rise up, pointing her bony finger and kill me with a single glance. She would curse me. She would take me prisoner and drag me down with her to curl forever in the seashell deep. The piles were alive, creaking softly, like the grim walls of a palace.

In the front room where I first saw the curled-up figure, I flashed my light into the gap between the furniture. Nothing now; just an old fireplace and a rolled-up carpet. I shrank back to the hallway. Faint light was coming from up above, muffled sounds.

Upstairs then.

I switched my torch off and changed to the

camera. Old faded stair carpet. An obstacle course of things on every step: wobbly-looking piles of books, shoes, a bike saddle. One step. Two. Phone clammy in my hand. Soft pant of my breath. As I neared the door of the upstairs room, someone started coughing. Panic swelled inside me. I must take the photo the minute the door was open. Should I shout something? "Surprise!"

They don't want any callers, the woman at the Co-op had said.

I pushed the door. I glimpsed a chair and, beside it, a sofa… a figure stretched out. I held my phone up. I pointed. *Click click click* lighting up the room.

"Is that you, Molly?" the figure murmured, turning over.

Click click for luck.

I dived behind the chair, scrolled to Lydia's number and sent the photo. **Here it is**, I texted.

I slid back to the door and out on to the landing. My hand wouldn't stop shaking. I dropped the phone, scrabbled around to pick it up, looked down. Molly was coming up the stairs, carrying a plate and mug. Her face changed. She glared up at me. "Ella?"

"I... I... wanted to see you," I said.

Her eyes narrowed. "Why are you in my house?" Her eyes fell on the phone between my hands. I cupped my fingers over it.

The hoarse voice called from inside the room. "Molly, love, is that you?"

"I'm coming," Molly called and then, to me, "Wait in the kitchen."

There in the dark at the top of the stairs, I clicked on the photo I had sent to Lydia. My screen showed a figure lying on a sofa, not curled up like last time, hair all standing out like bits of crazy wire... A woman... chalky thin face... trailing black dressing-gown thing, long white fingers. Under her eyes, bags of grey. Medicines and bottles and plates around her. My mind lurched.

Molly's mum looked... *sick.*

Chapter 18
Camera's
Truth

Dear Dad,

Mum says it's the turn of the year. The leaves are falling. I remember when you and me and Jack raked them all into a massive pile in our garden last year and then we all ended up having a leaf fight and falling in a heap laughing. Do you remember that, Dad?

Love, Ella

 xxx

What had I done?

I'd sent Lydia a photo of a sick, sad woman. Molly must be trying to look after her. Why would anyone want a photo of someone's mum like that?

It was wrong.

Molly's voice carried from inside the room, urging her mum to eat. "I brought you some toast," she was saying.

I felt as if a great wave was washing over me. I thought about Lydia. All the things she'd told me to do – they were always about Molly. But Molly hadn't done anything to Lydia, just ignored her. And I remembered how Lydia had made me feel about my eczema at her sleepover, the way she treated all her friends.

I found my way back down the stairs to the kitchen and clicked on Lydia's number. "I'm inside Molly's house," I whispered when she answered.

She giggled. "Oh, Ella. Get out!"

My voice came out strong. "Lydia, you have to delete the picture I just sent."

There was a little pause. "Go home, Ella," she said.

My phone went dead.

I texted her. **Delete the photo. Don't show it**

to anyone. It was a bad thing to do.

I waited for Molly. When she came in, I held out the stripy notebook. "I brought you this," I said. "For your drawing."

Molly sighed. She turned the bright notebook between her fingers. "I told you not to come in," she said. She sounded very tired.

"I'm sorry," I said. "I understand now."

Molly went to the sink and put the plate and cup in the washing-up bowl.

"That's your mum, isn't it? You told me she was busy collecting furniture and—"

Molly interrupted. "Mum's not well." She looked down into the sink. "Can I tell you, Ella? I feel as if I can but I don't want you to talk to anyone else."

No wonder Molly didn't trust me.

I had another thought, too. When I told Lydia about Dad, I'd felt ashamed of him, worrying that if people found out they wouldn't like me. Did Molly feel ashamed about her mum too?

"Tell me," I said.

"Dad used to have a shop. He knew lots of people. Mum was always different: shy, not going out much. Dad had an accident in our car and he was killed. That was more than a year ago. Since then, Mum won't leave the house at all. I've tried to persuade her, but she just won't."

"Is all the furniture and pots and things from your dad's shop?"

"Yes. It's closed. Mum said she would sort through and sell it all but she never has."

"So *you* buy all the food, look after her. You do all of it?"

"We'll be all right." Molly's jaw jutted. She clenched her fists. "Mum *will* get better again. I bought her some medicines."

"Does anyone else know?"

"They mustn't." Molly's voice turned fierce. "They would take Mum away. Put me in care. I've heard about it. The day you came and had the lemonade, you were the first person for a whole year."

I stared at Molly, full of horror. I hadn't come to be her friend that day – I had come to spy. How lonely she must be, on her own with her mum. How miserable. Not having anyone at school, not having a friend to tell all this time. I knew how that felt… to not have a friend. To lose your dad. But my dad would come back to us. Molly didn't even have that. My head reeled.

"On Sunday, please will you come round to my house?" I said. "Get what your mum needs then come round, whenever you want."

Molly smiled. "Thank you," she said. "Yes, I will."

Chapter 19
A Friend
for Tea

Dad,
Have you stopped writing to me? Are you cross with me?
Please write to me again.
Ella

On Saturday I told Mum I had invited a friend round, and on Sunday afternoon Molly came.

I texted Lydia. **You have deleted the photo, haven't you? I will explain on Monday. Ella**

I sent the message twice.

I didn't know how the visit would be. Molly was so quiet. What would we say to each other? The bad feelings about Lydia and the spying swirled inside me. *Start again with a new Ella...* I didn't know who Ella was any more. I just knew I felt so bad about Molly.

When our doorbell rang, Molly was on the step in a brown tracksuit that looked too small and I felt strange bringing her into my house. But she seemed really excited.

She looked at the star charts that Mum had made on the fridge, while we had a drink.

I am trying hard not to fight with Jack.

I am trying hard not to scratch my hands or rub the backs of my knees against hot surfaces.

I am trying hard to be polite.

I am trying hard to look after my new phone, collect it from the office and not gloat about it to Jack.

Signed Ella

"What happens when the gold stars reach the end?" Molly asked.

"Mum'll let me choose something," I said.

"Like a present?"

"Yeah, but we're always fighting and Mum keeps unpeeling my stars. She doesn't unpeel Jack's though."

Molly kept lightly touching things: the plants along the windowsill in their bright spotty pots, the tea and coffee canisters. "Your house is very smart," she said. We paused by the lounge with its big floppy sofas. Jack was on the computer by the window.

"Worm," he said without turning round.

"Worm yourself." I slammed the door. "That was my brother."

"Do you all sit in there?" Molly asked, as we went upstairs.

"Not often. Mum's always working. But if we watch a film, we do. Come on!"

Molly hung back in the doorway of my room. "I like all the colours," she said.

"Come in," I said.

"Can I sit down?" Molly gazed around at the two large posters on my walls, one of elephants at sunset and the other of clowns. The clown one was from Jack's room. I'd used it to cover the space left by Operation 13 being all torn off and pushed in a drawer. How horrible to think of all the ideas I'd had, pretending to be a police enquiry. I wished I could give Molly a present, make everything better.

"I like the red ladybird," she said, picking up my furry cushion.

I thought of Lydia holding it, sitting right there on my bed, making me tell her…

"If I had a bedroom like this, I'd never come out," Molly said.

I laughed. Molly laughed too.

"Have you always had eczema?" she asked, staring at the bottles and creams by my bed.

"Yes," I said, "but sometimes it's worse. Mum's making me try out some new ointment."

Molly smiled at me. "I only noticed you had it a few days ago."

"Really?"

"Will it go away?"

"I don't know."

"You probably think people are looking at it when they aren't really," she said.

Mum called us down for tea and we all sat round the table. Mum had made one of her strange new recipes with lots of red and yellow peppers on the top. Jack said "yuck" under his breath and Mum shot him a furious look.

"So, tell us about your family, Molly," Mum said.

Molly's face filled with dismay. She looked at me.

"There's just Molly and her mum," I said quickly. "And her mum's always busy."

Mum grinned. "I know that feeling."

Even though Molly was an extra person for tea, somehow the kitchen seemed quieter with her in it.

Jack whined, "Why haven't I got a friend round?"

There's a bar in the middle underneath the table and if you aim just right, you can stamp the other person's foot off. We're always doing it. Today, Jack kicked my foot off and I stamped on his and Molly just silently ate.

"Now, you two, that's enough," Mum said, loading salad on to her plate. "You had Sammy yesterday, Jacko."

"There's no one to play football with," Jack

whined again.

"I'll play," said Molly. Her smile lit up her face.

I stopped eating.

"Will you?" asked Jack. "Mum's always busy and Ella hates football."

I went to stamp his foot off again but Jack had already got up to clear the plates. Jack never cleared the plates.

Mum's meal was even weirder than usual but Molly seemed to love it, even some little curled-up things that looked like rice but weren't. Mum told Molly the whole recipe. "It's so nice to see someone who loves their food. Ella and Jack can be a bit picky. You need to watch the quantities of garlic in this one," she said. "And don't fry the onion, sweat it."

"Molly's got a rabbit," I said.

Jack's mouth fell open. "A rabbit...? How old is he...? How big...? What's his name?" He and Molly disappeared outside with him just going on and on asking about Nelson.

I went out too. Molly was running up and down the garden, winning the ball off Jack and hammering it into the goal. I was goalie for a while then I wandered away and sat on the bench.

Molly looked like a giant playing against Jack; her legs were so long.

"Goal!" they shouted each time one of them scored. Sometimes, when Molly tackled Jack, she would lift him right off the ground and his legs would still be bicycling and they'd fall on to the grass, giggling and tickling each other. I might as well not have been there. I kept watching them, thinking, he's horrible Jack – how come we're playing with him?

"Jack's really fun," Molly said when the game was over. "You're lucky. I don't have anyone else."

We only spoke about her mum once, when we were sitting in the garden on our own watching a squirrel raiding the bird table.

"What does your mum do all day?" I asked her.

"Before she got ill, she listened to the radio… sorted through my dad's stuff."

"Do you think your mum might like to open a shop? There must be valuable things in the piles, mustn't there?" I said.

Molly sighed. "I don't know. I just wish she'd get better and make some meals and stop crying."

The squirrel was hanging upside down now, calmly turning a nut in its claws. I was glad there was something to watch.

"I didn't know your mum cried," I said.

Molly bit her lip. "Well, she does. She can't help it."

How horrible to be crying all the time and not be able to stop. If Jack and I fought and he cried, Mum always took his side, even if the whole fight had been his fault. He only had to switch the tears on and the stupid big sobs and she would make us both apologise. Then Jack would stop, like turning off a tap. And Mum practically never cried. She just sniffed and sighed and said you had to move on. Like the day Dad got taken away. "I don't want to talk about it" was all Mum would say, staying strong and busy.

A grown-up who couldn't stop crying sounded like a nightmare!

"But your mum is getting better, isn't she?" I asked.

"She just needs to eat more. I've bought loads of medicines," Molly said. She looked at her watch. "I'd better go now. Can I come again?"

"Of course." I watched her from the door as she sprinted home on her long lanky legs.

While I soaked my hands that evening and rubbed in my creams, I thought about Molly Gardener, the things she'd said, her quiet ways. She'd talked about eczema as a small annoying thing. It wasn't that she didn't care; she just hadn't noticed. Maybe she was right. Maybe other people didn't really notice much either. Lydia had made me feel miserable about my eczema, but being with Molly made it seem just like a part of life.

I wondered how Molly's mum was today in their gloomy house. Maybe she was up and dressed already. Maybe Molly was having tea with her and they were both listening to some music on the radio.

Lydia would understand that I'd changed my mind, when I explained about Molly's mum tomorrow. I'd get to school early. I'd find her before anyone else. I'd make everything all right.

Chapter 20
Alone

Dear Dad,

Mrs Reynolds saw me give some chicken to Smokey and she said, "He knows which side his bread is buttered, that cat." But it was chicken, not bread. I think she means Smokey has an easy life. But it's not easy for birds. Half an hour later he caught a little bird under the tree and he wouldn't let it go; each time it did a little flap he batted it with his paw but when we tried to take it away from him he hissed. So it died. Mrs Reynolds just shook her head and said "It's a cat's way." Jack cried and cried. I really hated Smokey, just for a while. He is such a nice cat, so why is he mean? Jack said, "If Dad was here, he would have saved it."

You haven't answered about the money. Is that why you have stopped writing to me? Please write to me again even if it's just about boring things – I won't mind.

Please, Dad.

Love, Ella

I was going to set off early for school next day to find Lydia, but when I came out on to the step, Molly was waiting for me with her bike. "Can we go together?" she asked.

Mum smiled. "That's fine Ella, love. Just go across the recreation ground and keep off the road."

I got my bike out and waved goodbye to Mum and Jack. We set off. Inside I started panicking. How could I talk to Lydia if Molly was with me?

I wanted to make things all right. They nearly were.

I dashed into Willow class while Molly was changing her reading book. Lydia was on her own on the carpet. "The photo," I gasped. "You have deleted it, haven't you?"

Lydia smiled up at me. "Of course not."

I froze. "But I asked you to," I said. "I should never have taken it."

"Well, it's too late now," Lydia said calmly.

I stood there, reeling. "Lydia, you can't show it to anyone. Molly's mum's ill. It's not funny. She's a real person!"

"Well, I think it's funny."

"But…"

Lydia's laugh chimed out. "And Sophie will. And Rachel. And Immy. Hilarious!"

"You've sent it to them?" I said. "I said definitely not to..."

Lydia grinned her horrible smile. "You're not as brave as I thought."

"This isn't brave. It's just wrong."

How had I ever liked Lydia Sheridan? She looked like a monster to me now, a cruel monster. She waved me away as if she was swatting a fly. "Criminella was really the right name for you. Or Evil-hand Ella, that would be good, cos that's all you do, scratching your hands."

I stood there, *Evil-hand Ella*... little bullets piercing me, moving in and in.

✗

No one had their phone with them in the classroom. I had to wait all day. I had to sit next to Molly, listen to her, eat my lunch with her, all the time with the truth burning ... the picture I'd taken sent from phone to phone. In a hot panic I waited, watching Lydia, watching the others. Who had Lydia sent my photo to? And the worst thought: what if Molly saw it?

We'd said we'd cycle home. She didn't talk to

anyone else.

I had to keep her away from the others at the end of school.

I called out to Molly that I'd find her by the bike shed and dashed to get my phone the minute Mr Hales let us out. When I got to the office, a crowd of milling parents and children were all busy by the window asking the secretary questions. The air was full of complaining and shouting. Little kids with scooters had come in. Infants were being collected. I stood in the queue for phones. Come on, come on! I wanted to shout. I asked for my phone, grabbed it.

Giggles sounded around me. Sophie... Rachel... Immy. They had picked up their phones too, switched them on.

I had to get out.

Immy wandered right in front of me, staring at her phone. "Hey, Ella, have you seen this? Looks like a clown. Looks like a crazy grey clown with rats' tails for hair."

I had to get away.

I pushed against the crowd. Murmurs of irritation rose, a gap opened up.

"I came to find you!" Molly, coming through

the gap towards me.

"Molly!"

Immy dropped her phone and Molly bent to pick it up from between her feet. She looked at the screen. She stiffened, looked again, stared at me then slowly handed back Immy's phone.

Immy stared at Molly, then at me. Her mouth dropped open.

Molly turned, pushed her way back to the doors. Disappeared.

✗

I cycled to Molly's house.

I tried her front door. No answer.

I banged on her gate.

"Please, Molly. You must let me explain. Please!"

Molly's voice, when it came, had a terrible cold calm about it. "Did you take that photo in my house?"

"Molly, Lydia told me to do it."

"You sent it to *her*? Was it for a joke?" The fury in Molly's voice was unmistakable. "Imagine if it was your mum. I'm trying to look after her and you've ruined everything. You don't care – you're just selfish. Now everyone will know and they'll take her away. Or me. I should never have trusted you, Ella."

"But I didn't mean for this to happen," I sobbed.

"Go away. I don't want to know you," Molly said. "You are a bad person. I wish I'd never met you."

Chapter 21
All Kinds
of Stubborn

Dad,

When I do a bad thing, sometimes I wish I could start again.

I wish you were here, Dad. Why did you have to go away? Everything would be all right if you hadn't gone away.

I don't think I'm a photographer any more. It was a stupid idea.

Ella

When Mum came to get me up for school next morning I told her I wasn't well.

Mum's cool fingers rested on my forehead. She frowned. "You're not hot," she said. "What's wrong?"

"I'm just… quite ill," I said. I closed my eyes and lay very still.

The cool hand went. I peeped out.

Mum had started picking up my trousers and socks. "Ella, I can't take time off work; I've only just started. And Mrs Reynolds did lots of extra days over half-term." She laid all my uniform on the end of my bed. "You'll just have to go in and have a rest when you get home." She pushed back her hair. "Look, love, I'm trying to look after you and Jack. You have to be grown-up sometimes even if you don't feel great." She was at the door. "How about a pizza at the weekend?"

A big sob rolled inside me. "I wish we'd never come to this house," I said.

Mum turned. "There's no point wishing things like that." Her voice had a dangerous angry mum waiting in it. "Up you get, young lady!"

✗

None of Lydia's group spoke to me at school. I

didn't care about them anyway. I didn't care if I had to work with joking boys or with Bryony. Anyway, Bryony was the only girl who had no idea what was going on. The only important thing was that Molly was off school. When Mr Hales called her name out, there was a hush and someone said, "Maybe she's tidying her room," and my class laughed and I felt bad. Everyone must know about the inside of Molly's house now. I sat by myself in the playground by the railings where Molly always sat sketching in her notebook.

I went to art club and worked on my own. Lydia didn't come. I kept thinking of the mountain maze and a lonely sad girl wandering through it, so worried about her mum that she didn't dare leave her. Taking photos just made me think of the horrible picture I'd taken. What if one of the teachers saw my photo? Molly was right; I was a bad friend. I was a liar and a cheat. I remembered when they took Dad away – the quiet in our house and Jack waking in the night and clinging to me, asking if Mum would go away and leave us too.

When I got home with Mrs Reynolds and Jack I felt glad to do homework and read and not think about the mess I'd made. Jack couldn't wind me up. Each time he said something mean or when he took the last biscuit, I just said, "Go away. I don't care what you do." He even threw a duvet down the stairs and it landed on my head. I saw his face, full of glee. But I just rolled the duvet up and carried it back upstairs to the cupboard on the landing.

"You're no fun!" Jack wailed.

Mrs Reynolds offered me an extra biscuit, saying, "You look like a wet weekend, sweetheart." I felt the tears start in my eyes, sniffed and wiped my nose on the tissue she handed me.

"Do you want to tell me about it?" she asked, laying her cool dry hand over mine. "Have you had an argument?"

I sniffed and gulped. "Kind of," I said.

"Girls can be very unkind," she said.

My tears spilled out then. The unkind person was me.

She patted my hand. "Now, now, it can't be that bad."

"It is." I gulped. "I did something so mean." I couldn't say any more words.

"Then make it right. Apologise. Life's too short to let these things roll on." Mrs Reynolds' face was full of concern. "Can I tell you something? There's all kinds of stubborn. If you know you are in the wrong, you should always say sorry. My husband could never bring himself to do it, bless him. If we had an argument, he'd let it run on for days. But it does no good."

"I've tried," I said. "She won't listen."

Mrs Reynolds smiled. I wished she wouldn't smile. She didn't understand how bad this was if she could smile like that.

"Keep trying," she said briskly. "Now how about peeling some carrots? I thought we'd make a casserole for your mum. She's a wonder, all those hours she's putting in at work."

I thought of the lists and the rules on the fridge and how Mum made me feel safe. I know she got cross and she didn't have much time to spend with me and Jack, but I didn't worry about her. I thought about Molly – she must feel as if life might go wrong every minute. She didn't have a mum who wrote lists and sorted everything out.

I had to try again to say sorry. I'd done a terrible thing. Mrs Reynolds was right. I had to make things better.

Chapter 22
In the
Maze Again

Dad,
Why don't you write to me?

While Mrs Reynolds was shouting answers at the TV I let myself quietly out and went down the road to Molly's. A faint light was still on in the upstairs window. The rest of the house was dark. I tried the back gate. Locked. I took the route over the fence, half climbing half falling over the top. I tried not to think of Molly's furious face.

I went inside and weaved my way through the piles, waving away webs, round furniture, not stopping this time, upstairs. I pushed the bedroom door open.

Around the sofa, bottles, drinks, plates and cups lay scattered. A smell like curdled milk hung in the air.

Molly was sitting beside her mum. She turned and her raggedy black hair fell over her eyes.

"I know you don't want to see me," I said. "I just came to say sorry."

"Just go away, Ella." Molly's voice wasn't angry, more far away. She stroked her mum's forehead as if she wasn't thinking about me any more.

I listened to the coughing. The first time I'd spied and heard coughing must be three weeks ago. Molly's mum had been sick for ages, I realised.

The woman's face looked bluish grey. The dark circles under her eyes looked like hollows. Her hands flopped, grasped at nothing. She definitely looked… different. When she breathed, her breaths just seemed to be little gasps. Last time I came she wasn't like that, I was sure. And wasn't that just how Grandad had sounded when he was really ill in hospital?

The sweet sick smell filled my nose. What if this illness was serious? I remembered Mrs Reynolds saying there's all kinds of stubborn. Molly was a stubborn person, deciding never to talk to Lydia. What if she had decided her mum would get better with the medicines from the Co-op and stuck to that idea too?

"I will go. I'll do whatever you want, Molly, but I'm worried. Can your mum breathe all right?" I asked.

I remembered Grandad gripping my hand, the rasping noise of his breathing. "Molly, my grandad sounded like this when he was really ill. He had nurses all around him and machines checking him and he was in hospital."

Molly's face was full of fury now. "Mum isn't that bad. She just needs to eat, get strong."

Molly's mum had a bout of coughing – small, dry, barking sounds.

"What if you're wrong? What if she needs experts?"

"Just go."

"I know you don't want your mum to leave the house but I think she could be really ill. She could die, Molly."

"You don't know anything!" Molly thundered.

Her mum's head hardly moved now, as if she didn't have the energy to even cough. Her eyes rolled with a kind of far-away glassy look.

My whole body was shaking. "Please, Molly. We need to call an ambulance!"

A huge tear rolled down Molly's cheek. "I can't let them take her away…"

I put my arms round Molly and hugged her. "We have to help her, Molly. We have to do it now."

Molly pulled away from me and sank down to hold her mum's hand. She did a tiny nod.

I pulled out my phone and dialled.

"Which service do you require?" a voice asked.

"Ambulance," I said. "Please can you send an ambulance…? Number 13 Ash Grove."

I left them together and walked downstairs to meet the ambulance, out in the crisp evening air.

Maybe I was wrong. Well, if I was, the ambulance people would tell me off and say I was wasting their time. They would go away and I'd get in trouble. I'd explain. For the first time in a long time I felt like me.

I rang home. "Mrs Reynolds, I popped down the road to check on my friend and they're sending an ambulance," I said.

"Whatever have you done, Ella?" Mrs Reynolds cried.

"Nothing," I said. "It's Molly's mum. She's really sick. Please will you come? Jack knows where."

I stood by the gate so the ambulance would see me.

I heard the siren from far away. When I saw the flashing light, I waved my arms above my head and the ambulance stopped. Two people in green suits sprang out. "There's a lady upstairs who keeps coughing. I think she might be really ill," I told them.

I didn't go inside. I heard them explaining to Molly at the kitchen door, saying, "We just want to check that your mum's all right."

A few minutes later they came dashing out and collected a stretcher. It took them a long time to come out again. There were crashes and furniture-moving noises inside the house.

Two figures appeared, coming down the road towards me – Mrs Reynolds wobbling along, gripping Jack's arm.

The back door banged and the ambulance people appeared, carrying the stretcher between them. Molly's mum had a mask on her face and Molly walked beside her. Molly climbed inside the ambulance and looked out at me with a face so miserable I had to look away. "This is it," she seemed to say. "You have made them take my mum, Ella Mackay!"

"I've not walked so fast in years," Mrs Reynolds said, appearing beside me.

"She did," echoed Jack. "She hardly used her stick at all."

Mrs Reynolds bustled round to the door and spoke to the ambulance people, then the doors slammed with Molly and her mum inside.

"Can you tell me about it now, love?" Mrs Reynolds said, putting her arm round me. "I'd like to understand."

Through my tears I told her what I knew about Molly's mum. She watched me gravely.

"Well, you shouldn't be too hard on yourself for calling the ambulance," she said. "They suspect the poor lady has pneumonia. You've probably saved her life."

Chapter 23
The Long
Dark Car

Dad,
I keep remembering. I can't stop it.
Molly's face staring out at me.
The slam of the ambulance doors.
It made me remember when those people took
you away...

A dark long car that isn't our car. I can smell the inside car-seat smell even though I'm outside on the street.

The doors slam closed. CLUMP. The voices stop.

He's in the back. The passenger seat is empty.

Two people, a man and a woman, one each side of him and a driver. That's because he needs a person on either side so he doesn't run away. That's how you know he's a prisoner and not just a person getting a lift.

Dad sitting very straight in the middle. Dad's head facing forward, not turning. On his knees, the carrier bag he brought downstairs.

He doesn't wave. I wish he would wave. I wish the two people would turn and talk to him. He could tell them about us, about me and Jack. "I've got a girl and a boy," he could say. "Don't keep me away too long. I need to get home to them."

Mum doesn't get up. She sits in the lounge with a straight back staring at the window. She doesn't even say goodbye.

The headlights are on – their beams jutting out across the backs of all the parked cars. The smooth swish of the car pulling away.

✗

When Mrs Reynolds and Jack and I got back home after seeing the ambulance leaving, I didn't want to talk to Mum. But there she was, just back from work, standing in the hall with her organised face. My insides twisted.

"Sylvia tells me you've been upset about your friend. What's happened, Ella?"

I couldn't lie to Mum. Not after today. Not now. My eyes welled up. "I... I... another girl, Lydia, told me to... spy on Molly," I said.

Mum frowned. "What do you mean, *spy*?"

"Find out things. Lydia made me watch Molly's house and take photos and then I took a photo inside and found out her mum was really ill. Oh, Mum, it was so wrong... and, and..." The tears came thick and strong.

Mum took hold of my shoulders, gently, staring into my face. "I don't understand, Ella. How could another girl make you do something like that?"

"She, Lydia... she... she said she'd tell other people... about Dad."

Mum took a sharp breath. "She knows about your dad? You told her about Dad? Ella, how could you?"

The sobs came, louder, bigger. I sank down on to the bottom stair. "Lydia asked lots of questions until I told her. That day when she gave me the party shoes, she'd worked out that I had a secret and she saw you and Jack and she just went on asking, *Is it about your dad?* And I told her and I'm so sorry." I curled away from Mum. "I'm so, so sorry."

I couldn't help the words coming now. "I can't forget about Dad. I can't pretend he's not our dad. I know you don't want to talk to us about him but… he's always in my head." Shuddering sobs shook me. I had no more voice left.

"Oh, Ella," I heard Mum saying, "I've been so stupid. How awful. I didn't understand, love."

And then Mum's arms were round me and her face burrowing into my hair and hugging and hugging me and all the sadness pouring out of us until there were no more tears left to cry.

Dear Molly,
If you don't answer this message, I will leave you alone. I am very sorry for taking the photo. I hope your mum is feeling better.

Please can we start again?
Love, Ella

✗

It was Saturday morning, only three days since Molly and her mum had left in the ambulance. "I can't go," I said from my bed. "It's a stupid idea."

"I think you should," Mum said, standing in my doorway. "I've checked the visiting times."

"I can't talk to her. Anyway, I sent a message and she never replied."

How could Mum even ask me to go to the hospital? I shouldn't be anywhere near Molly. Never. No way.

"She may not have got your message."

Why didn't Mum just leave me alone? "She won't want me. Stop nagging me!"

"Ella, that girl's on her own. Imagine how you would feel."

I couldn't imagine it. It all felt bad and wrong and terrible. And the most terrible bit of it was me.

I humphed and rolled and lay still. I closed my eyes.

"Well, Jack and I will go," Mum said.

My door swished shut. I heard Mum's feet on

the stairs and she called, "Jack!"

I jumped off the bed. "But you and Jack don't really know Molly," I called, following her down.

Mum had her keys in her hand. "You'd better come with us then. Just get dressed and put your trainers on."

We drove into the car park. "The least you can do is say hello," Mum said.

The hospital felt hot and stuffy. There were so many corridors; I couldn't imagine ever getting out. It smelled of cleaning and medicine. Nurses and patients walked around, looking for where they were supposed to be. As I followed Mum and Jack, I kept thinking about how strange the hospital must be for Molly's mum after being inside a mountain maze. My feet felt heavy. I had lead boots. Dread boots. I had a lot to say to Molly and nothing at all, all at once.

When we got to the ward, we weren't allowed to see Molly's mum at all because she was too ill. Molly was sitting outside the room on a blue plastic chair, in her brown tracksuit.

Molly's long legs swung as she stared through grey glass.

I stopped dead.

"Come on," Mum said. "Hello, Molly."

Jack called, "Molleee!" and dashed towards her.

Molly turned. She didn't smile at us. Mum crossed the wide grey floor. I kept behind her. My insides turned to jelly.

A nurse came out to shush Jack and for a moment I saw the side of a bed and a hand and tubes going down beside it. Machines beeped. The door closed.

"I was only saying hello," Jack whined.

We stood there.

Mum spoke to the nurse. *"In isolation, yes... very worried... out of danger... yes... yes..."*

"Can I take Molly down to the café?" Mum waved towards Molly.

"Good idea," the nurse said. "I'll keep an eye on your mum, Molly."

Molly nodded, stood up and followed Mum and Jack.

I came last.

I remembered how Molly seemed to carry silence with her, when she came for tea, last weekend ... before ... just before.

Mum bought us drinks and biscuits in the café.

There was a children's play area outside. Molly drifted over to it to sit on a hump shaped like a bee. It stuck out on a sort of coil to make the bee bounce. I don't think Molly was expecting that.

She wobbled and fell off.

Jack got on the one next to her: an ant with waving legs. He wobbled it, holding the front pair of feelers, plunging down and up, wobbling and bouncing.

Molly climbed back up on hers.

"Mine's a flying one!" Jack shouted.

He and Molly bounced. I watched. Then Jack fell off his and went to get a biscuit.

I climbed on his. "Did you get my message?" I asked Molly, sitting there, holding on.

"Don't talk about it," Molly said. She bounced on the bee and the bright sun poured down on her face.

We both bounced.

Jack rushed over, shouting, "Are you on the moon yet?"

Molly smiled at him. "Nearly!"

I climbed off and let him have a go again.

I collected drinks for Molly and me from the picnic table where Mum sat flicking through the messages on her phone.

I flopped down to sit beside Molly. "I'm really sorry," I said.

Chapter 24
I Know
Everything
About You

Dear Dad,

That's a big, big shame that you can't have a holiday from being in prison.

I didn't know you were sorry. I didn't know you felt bad about the stealing every minute of every day. Don't worry, Dad. You got in a tangle. I've been in a tangle too, Dad.

Lots of love, Ella

 xxx

The days passed slowly. I sat in the class on my own, with Bryony, ignoring everyone and visiting Molly at hospital after school.

There are lots of kinds of stubborn. I found a new kind inside me. I ate my sandwiches outside every day on the wall. I ignored Lydia's group. I pretended they were invisible.

I even stopped wearing the hot green jumper when our classroom was warm, and left my sore arms bare.

One lunchtime, as I walked past them all on my way outside, Rachel called out in front of everyone. "Ella, is Molly OK?"

I stopped.

Lydia, Rachel, Sophie, Immy, Hannah, Zing. They were all there.

"Molly's all right," I said.

"Someone said her mum's in hospital," Immy said.

"Yes," I said. "She's very ill."

"Oh."

Silence.

"Molly's mum has pneumonia," I said.

"What's that?" asked Lydia.

"It's an illness. It means it's hard to breathe.

Molly had been trying to look after her."

"What, in *that mess*?" Lydia almost spat the words.

Everyone looked at Lydia.

"Why are you always so mean about Molly?" Rachel asked.

"It's because of the art competition," Immy said. "It's because Molly won it, isn't it? Last term."

"I don't know what you mean!" snapped Lydia.

I looked round the group. An art competition. Before I arrived. It was all starting to make sense. Hot anger rose inside me. "So, Molly's dad's accident last year – did you all know about that?"

"Yes. The teachers told our whole class," Rachel said.

I gaped at Rachel. "You mean, there never was a mystery."

Everyone was waiting for Lydia now.

"I think you're all being horrid," she said at last.

Angry words burst out of me. "You made me keep investigating just to hurt Molly!"

Lydia had a cold smile. "There's plenty more people I could hurt if I wanted to, Ella Mackay." She pointed her long white finger at me. "I know lots of things about you, don't forget."

My hands clenched. "No you don't. Not really."

A tray clattered at the other end of the lunch hall.

I gulped. I felt all eyes on me. "My dad got put in prison for doing a bad thing." My voice came out loud. "He's really sorry for what he did. He feels bad every day."

A chair scraped. Silence.

"My dad made a mistake. He's making up for it. People should say sorry when they do a bad thing." I stared into Lydia's blue, blue eyes. "Don't you think a person should say sorry when they do a bad thing, Lydia?"

I stared around at Lydia's open-mouthed friends. Lydia looked down at the table, her smile quivering.

I realised I didn't care. I'd said the secret, mine and Mum's and Jack's. She couldn't do anything to me. The thought rose up like a cheer inside me. "I'll still have friends," I told her. "They'll be people who don't lie and cheat. People like Molly!"

I headed for the door, my words roaring inside my head, and plunged out into the playground, half sobbing.

But then a noise came from behind me. "Hey, Ella." I turned to see Immy. "Say hi to Molly for me," she said. "Say I hope her mum's better soon."

I nodded.

"Maybe you could come over for tea sometime?" Immy said. "If you want to."

I grinned. "I'd love that. Thanks!"

✗

Once Molly's mum was definitely getting better, Mum took me to meet her one day after school. I didn't want to, but I knew I had to.

"This is Ella, Mum," Molly said.

A woman in a pale blue dressing gown was in a hospital chair looking out of the window. Her dark hair was brushed and flat and she had a wide pale face like Molly's. She looked sleepy, not scary. Molly was holding on to her mum's hand.

"Hello, Ella," her mum said softly.

A wave of hot shame pulled me down. What could I say?

Molly stroked her mum's forehead. "Ella's the one who called the ambulance." Her voice was flickery and gentle, as if they both spoke a special rare language. She turned back to me. "Mum gets tired," she said.

My own mum was waiting in the doorway. Now she came in and said hello. "I'm so glad our girls are getting to know each other."

You shouldn't be; I'm a bad person who nobody trusts, I thought.

But Mum put her arm round me and beckoned Jack in from the corridor. Jack zoomed in, making his aeroplane noise. Molly's mum smiled.

"Can we play football?" he asked Molly. "Please!"

Mum laughed. "Jack, it's a hospital."

"I'll play carefully," he said.

And then we were all laughing, apart from Jack, who stood there in the middle of the room, asking, "What's so funny?"

He stamped his foot. His face went naughty and cross and I thought, *Oh no!*

But then Molly suddenly said, "While Mum's in hospital, would you help to look after my rabbit, Jack?"

Jack's face lit up like Christmas. "Really?"

Chapter 25
Whisper it
to Me

Hi Dad,

My skin is bad. Mum says I'm scratching a lot at night and she's making me wear the scratch mitts again. Mrs Reynolds says the Queen wears gloves for her garden parties at Buckingham Palace. But those parties are in the daytime. And, anyway, my mitts are brown and splotchy and they smell really yuck, like vinegar, because of all the creams.

I do all the things like long sleeves and the washing and the soaking and the creams and all the food things. I hate not having ice cream when we go out. Every time we have the soya one at teatime I say I should have double because I've missed so many and Mum laughs. But I should! The doctor said my skin was angry. I keep thinking about eczema being a shouting thing but I think eczema is more like insects burrowing inside and trying to escape. I would like to unzip my skin and hang it up so I could go to bed without it, so all the itches would leave me alone. Then I'd be a skeleton. I'm going to tell that to Jack cos he really likes skeletons. Sometimes Mum holds my hands still and says "You've scratched enough." But it isn't like that. Even if I scratched all the skin off I think a little itch would find me.

Love, Ella

Molly was going to stay at our house while her mum was in hospital.

We made a bed for her in my room on the spare mattress. There wasn't any extra space to walk around; we were like peas in a pod, Mum said. The first night, Mum came in and kissed us both goodnight. "Not too much chatting or you'll never get up in the morning!"

The light flicked off and all the shapes in the room disappeared. I snuggled down. I was pleased Molly was here. In the quietness, I listened to the water pipes making their clanking noises on the landing.

But then a snuffling noise started. I listened. It turned to long, choking sobs.

"Molly," I whispered. "Are you all right?"

Some words I couldn't hear. Mum... Something about Mum? "What's wrong?"

"Your mum kissed me... She hugged me."

"I'll tell her not to. It's all right."

But Molly was sobbing again. "I don't want her to stop. She... nobody... nobody kisses me goodnight."

I stared down into the dark where Molly's voice was. "So, your mum doesn't...?"

"No... I always check *she's* OK. Then just... go to my bed... on my own."

"Oh!" A cold picture came into my head: Molly lying all still in a bed in her house.

A big gulp rose inside me. Mum always tucks us in. She doesn't really tuck – she just calls it tucking us in – and holds me, smelling of Mum: her jumper, her hair. "Oh, Molly, I'm so sorry your mum isn't... your mum can't..."

Molly's voice again. "I think Mum got too sad when Dad died. I think that made her go strange. I was scared sometimes. I don't think she knew what she was going to do. She was like Mum but ... somewhere else. I didn't tell anyone at school. I didn't want Mr Hales knowing things... He might think Mum was mad. She isn't mad, Ella."

Molly's voice turned into a whisper. "Sometimes I *did* think she was mad... like when she made a big mess in the kitchen and I got back from school and there were eggs everywhere and I got so angry and shouted at her and she just cried. *I wanted to make you a cake, Molly. I wanted it to be waiting when you got back but I couldn't make the eggs work...* I think the sadness was just making her brain wrong."

Molly was silent. The clanking noise from the pipes had stopped, and our house was very quiet. It seemed to wrap itself round me, warm. I couldn't bear thinking about the cake Molly's mum had tried to make.

"But she's getting better now?" I asked.

Molly sighed. "Yes. The tablets make her sleepy. She still cries a bit but she holds my hand more and looks at me and it's like... she can really *see* me now. And she asks me about school and my art. Before she had me Mum used to do art too; she was a painter."

"That's why you love art!"

"Yes. I don't know why Mum stopped. I'd like her to start again. And be happy."

Lying talking in the dark beside Molly was like talking to myself. I couldn't *see* her listening. "I've got something to tell you too," I said. "My dad's in prison. He stole some money." It was easy to tell Molly. "When he first got in trouble Mum went up to my school and talked to the headmistress, and I had to look after Jack in the playground and I kept wondering what they were saying. I knew it was bad though. I could hear Mum and Dad arguing when I was in bed. *How could you do something so stupid?* Mum kept saying. Dad was crying. *I did it for us.*

"Did you tell anyone?" Molly asked.

"No, only my friend Grace. I said that Dad was going to be in a big court case and she mustn't tell anyone and she just said, *Don't worry.* Dad kept hugging me and Jack so much."

"Who did he steal from?"

"The bank where he worked. The court was to decide how to punish him. It took a whole week. Dad said he was guilty right at the start. He said he needed the money to pay someone back and he hadn't told anyone, not even Mum. I think all my teachers knew by then. I hated them asking, '*Are you all right, Ella?*'"

"And your dad got taken away?"

"He's been in prison for six months but they're keeping him for three years."

Molly was quiet.

"After Dad went, a man jumped out from between the cars on our road waving a long camera when we had only just got back from the supermarket. *Mrs Mackay, do you have any comment?* and Mum screamed at me to *Get Jack inside and shut the curtains.* So we ran. And Mum was grabbing shopping bags and slamming the car doors and the man was rushing round taking pictures. It was like a hunt. And when he'd gone, we all sat at the bottom of the stairs while Mum cried. I thought it was just Dad who did the bad thing but I think some people thought it was Mum or they wanted to watch us and see if we were bad too. And when I was going to school, Mrs Griffiths opposite came out on her step and shook her doormat then stared at me really long and hard without saying hello or smiling. It was horrible, just looking down at my shoes till I heard her door slam. And Mum shouted at Grandma. *'I'm not staying here with everyone staring at us; I've not seen a penny of that money!'"*

I stopped.

The secret was gone, all smashed and gone away. I stared into the dark where Molly was. "I write to my dad," I told Molly. "I'll tell him you're my new friend."

Molly's gentle voice came again. "Do you go and visit him?"

"Mum doesn't want us to."

Molly sighed. "But he's your dad."

I lay in the warm, quiet dark and thought about

Dad: his face in a happy grin, Dad running around the garden with Jack on his shoulders, Dad chasing me on the beach on holiday.

Chapter 26
Cooking

Dad,
What do you do if you feel sad in prison?

"What is your dad like?"

"He likes doing funny things. We've got this joke: sometimes he used to make us a Pizza Jellybeana if we had a bad day at school or someone was fed up. Dad loves jellybeans. But the pizza can have anything on it: stupid things like fruit or sweets. When Jack fell off his bike and bashed his nose he had the hankie in one hand pressing his cut nose and did the toppings with the other." I smiled. "Dad says there's nothing so bad that a Pizza Jellybeana won't make it better."

"Could we make one?" Molly's voice came out of the dark.

I leaned up on one elbow. "Now?" I wanted to laugh.

"Well, your dad can't make one but *we could*."

Molly wasn't used to a grown-up checking. She did what she wanted.

I was sure I remembered a pizza in our freezer though, near the bottom. I started to grin. "OK then. Come on."

We found ourselves giggling at the door. "I'll talk to Mum. You just go down."

Molly padded away downstairs. I crossed over to Mum's room and eased the door open.

Mum was sitting in bed in her red pyjamas. She had the laptop on her knees and all the usual work papers in piles around her. "Ella! Are you all right, love?"

"I... I... Molly and me, we're both a bit hungry."

Mum's eyes went wide. "But you had a *huge* tea!"

I nodded. "We're just... hungry again. Could we go down and get a snack? We'll be quiet." I tried to make my face look ordinary and blank. "Maybe Molly needs to... build herself back up."

Mum nodded. "Some crackers or something?" She looked down at her laptop again. "Keep the noise down, though," she murmured.

"Thanks, Mum."

I pulled her door firmly shut and scurried away down the stairs.

The kitchen was lit up with warm orange light from the tiled bit over the oven.

"I put the oven on," Molly said.

Of course; she was used to cooking in her house.

I found the pizza at the bottom of the freezer and pulled it out of its packaging. It felt very light and cardboardy. "Mum's busy doing work things," I told Molly. "What shall we put on the pizza?"

We grinned at each other. "Everything!"

"Raisins… half an apple… marshmallows…?"

There are so many things you can put on a pizza.

"Shall we do a clown face?" Molly suggested.

"It always goes splurgy in the oven anyway," I said. "You never know how it's going to look."

We put halves of grapes for eyes with raisins pushed inside the marshmallows for hair. I raided Mrs Reynolds' fairy cake decorations: chocolate sprinkles and jelly fruit shapes.

"Chocolate flakes for eyebrows," Molly giggled, breaking up a bar and fanning it out.

"Banana mouth," I said, carefully slicing one.

"A whole mushroom for his nose."

"He looks like a pig in a wig." I thought of Dad and how much he would laugh. I felt as if he was with me, finding all the silliest things.

How about a peanut toffee coconut pizza?

No, Dad!

Molly put the pizza in the oven and we watched through the glass as the tomato started to ripple and the marshmallows rocked about.

Molly giggled. "It's bubbling... his eyes are exploding!"

The whole clown face was alive, popping like lava. An eye slid off and fizzed on the baking tray.

We poured glasses of squash and watched the face slide. Then, when the edge was going browner, Molly took the pizza out and laid it on the breadboard. We stared. Now our pizza looked like a planet with craters and strange lakes and coloured pools. The marshmallows were still bobbly and sticky when I poked them. We began to pull bits off.

Molly screwed up her nose and took a bite. "It tastes weird. I like the raisins... not so sure about the chocolate eyebrows."

"Have you tried a grape?" I giggled. "Grapes with tomato and a marshmallow on top. Dee-licious!"

We clinked our drinks together, Molly and me. It was like a birthday... our silly pizza day for Dad. "Let's always make Pizza Jellybeana!"

Then Mum was there in the doorway, all tousled in her pyjamas. "*What* are you two doing?" Her voice had a hard edge.

I looked at the mess of decorations on the

worktop: little heaps, bags lying open, sprinkles around the kettle. I leapt from my chair. "Sorry, Mum."

"Ella, this is—" Mum's voice stopped. She rubbed the back of her hand across her eyes and sat down on one of the chairs. "I see what you're doing…" Her voice sank to a whisper. "Ella…"

"It's all right, Mum. Please don't be angry. We'll clear it all up."

Mum's head sank down onto her hand. She sighed. "You made a Pizza Jellybeana." She smiled and held out her arms to hug me. "He would have loved it, Ella."

Chapter 27
Lists

Dad,

Jack's still playing that Sports Champ game you bought him and he said that if he gets a really high ranking he'll be much better than you when you get home – see, he does still think about you!

Guess what – Molly and me made Pizza Jellybeana.

When you come home, you'll be able to go on your mountain bike again, won't you, and have three scoops of ice cream?

Here's a picture of the bike and lots of ice-cream flavours for you to choose from.

Mum says hello.

Love, Ella

Some days Molly came with me to school, but other days she went to be with her mum and did extra schoolwork in the hospital with a special teacher. Molly's clothes smelled of our washing powder now. We moved Nelson's cage to our back garden and Jack took him all over the place, murmuring to him. We even discovered him in Jack's bedroom and Mum was very angry and said, "Never, never does that rabbit come in your room, do you understand me, young man?"

But I knew Mum was laughing inside because when she'd finished the telling off, she did a tiny smile at me. "He's got to learn," she whispered.

One evening, I sat in Mum's bed and I showed her the letters Dad had sent me. We talked quietly about the bad time before he got taken away.

When Molly's mum, Beth, had been in hospital for two weeks, we all went down to Molly's house to collect more rabbit food and bedding. Mum said we should check the house too. Mum, Jack, Molly and me let ourselves in.

"Right," Mum said, wedged up against an antique sink and staring up at the strange carved wardrobe in Molly's hall. The smell was worse:

damp and mouldy, like the inside of an old shed.

Molly went up to her bedroom to collect some more clothes she needed and Jack darted between mountains of furniture.

"There's just so much," Mum said in a voice that sounded very sad and shocked. "I just can't believe they've been living here. Beth can't come back home to this. She needs space… light."

When Molly came down, we all weaved through to the back of the house to find the rabbit bedding and Mum stared around the wild, tall garden. Jack threw himself into the grass, saying, "I can't find my legs. My legs have gone."

We went back to lock the house and Mum said very gently to Molly, "Molly love, do you think your mum really wants all these things?"

"Not any more." Molly shook her head. "She just wants to get better."

That evening, I waited until Molly was playing a computer game with Jack and helped Mum sort the washing.

"You said Molly's mum mustn't come home to all this stuff in the house, that it was making her miserable." I matched up a red and black stripy sock with its partner and made a ball. "So how will she get better then?"

Mum sighed. "It's great you want to help the Gardeners, Ella, really it is. Some things just have to be done slowly, that's all. And there may be other people who can help, people at the hospital. We mustn't be steamrollering them."

"But there must be something we can do *now* … and not be steamrollering?"

Mum folded a towel and smoothed it flat. "Molly's mum might have special memories about some of the furniture." She reached for another armful of washing. "Molly's the one we have to help. Why don't you try talking to her about it gently?"

So that night, when we were lying in bed, I said to Molly, "Is there anything we can do to help make your house nice for when your mum comes home again? But only if you want to…"

"There is something." Molly's voice was soft in the dark. "Mum said she would like us to make a list of all the things in the house."

"Of course," I said. "I'll ask Mum."

So we all went round to Molly's again at the weekend.

I made lists on a big sheet of paper – name of

room, type of object, what it was made of and, sometimes, the measurements. Mrs Reynolds had said she had a friend who knew about antiques and might be able to work out how much some of the things were worth.

Some of Jack's descriptions were really stupid, like 'monstrous sink' or 'smelly fireplace' so I ignored them. It was hard to remember which objects we had already done so I put our gold behaviour stickers on them. Then I had the idea of taking photos of all the bigger things so we could give the list to Molly's mum with a photo. "That way she's bound to realise some of the things are horrid and she doesn't want them," I whispered to Mum, when Molly had gone upstairs to her room.

We carried some of the smaller objects like stools and small cupboards outside into the back garden so we could see the big pieces of furniture properly.

Although Molly came back downstairs, she didn't really help us make the lists, just wandered about staring at the things. I wondered if maybe she was trying to work out which things she and her mum could sell to antique shops. Mum and I gradually moved from the door into the middle of the room, me calling things out and Mum writing them down and then doing measuring together.

Jack just went off exploring and calling, "This is a werewolf warehouse!"

We found Molly crouched down, rubbing the dust and cobwebs off something. "Dad loved this," she said quietly.

It was a domed box the size of our microwave, made of gleaming metal.

Jack popped out from behind the wardrobe. "What is it?"

"It's a cash register, isn't it?" Mum said, bending to look. "For taking the money, in the shop? It's lovely, Molly."

"Dad said it was a quality piece. It's the actual one from his shop," Molly said.

Together we lifted it onto a table. It smelled oily and some dark grease streaked on my sleeve.

The cash register was an old gold colour with a fancy curly top. The domed metal front had lots of buttons standing out. It didn't look a bit like the ones I'd seen in shops and supermarkets.

"I can be a shopkeeper!" Jack said.

"It's very grand," I said. "Try... thirty-one

pounds and twenty-six pence." Jack pressed the buttons down hard – *clack, clack, clack* – and the numbers popped up in the top window.

"You have to turn the handle," Molly murmured. "I remember doing this… a long time ago." She ran her fingers over the complicated metal designs on the side.

Jack wound the handle and there was a massive *ding* as the drawer flew open. "Look, there's even money inside." He scooped up some dark brown coins. "That was cool!" he said. "Let's do it again. Thank you, madam!"

Jack rang up some more charges. I tried all the buttons down one side. Some were quite stiff and the colours were flaking off but the cash register still felt very smart.

"We'll have to take the photos from the front and the side because they're both beautiful," I told Molly when Jack moved off to look at the rocking horse. "It's almost like a jewellery box. I don't know how much cash registers are worth. Maybe if I take a good photo after we clean it up, Mrs Reynolds' friend would look it up on the Internet and find out what it's worth and then we could…"

I stopped.

Molly was staring at me. "Leave it alone!" she snapped, her mouth wobbling. "I'm keeping it."

I realised with a horrid jolt that she was crying. Mum appeared behind Molly and just put her arms round her. "Shall we put it in your room, Molly?" she said. "Of course you should keep it."

And then Mum and Molly heaved the cash register between them and disappeared upstairs to Molly's room and I was left just standing there, on my own, in the middle of all the mess.

I gulped. A big lump had arrived in my chest. It pushed hard against me. Had I mucked everything up? Had I hurt Molly again?

Jack appeared with a huge basket and said, "I'm taking this," and disappeared outside.

Molly's and Mum's voices sounded again, coming downstairs.

"Molly's going outside for a while," Mum said as Molly disappeared off towards the kitchen like a shadow.

I helped Mum finish the lists for a bit longer. I wished I was with Molly but I stayed with Mum. I felt as if I might get everything wrong again if I went to see her. I might make her sad. It was better if I was just a list-making person who didn't talk about selling things. Soon Mum and I had labelled everything in the room and swept the floor so we could see the floorboards.

"Ella!" Molly's voice called from the kitchen. "We need you outside!"

She sounded different.

Mum grinned and stretched. "Well, go on, love, you've been brilliant. I could murder a cup of tea."

"I'm coming!" I called back.

I pushed open the back door to the garden. I blinked then gasped.

Spread out across the grass were a chimney pot on its side, shelves, pots, stools, even an old toilet, all making ramps and slopes, and Molly and Jack were beckoning me and waving.

Jack leapt and giggled. "Come and look! It's our amazing obstacle race. You climb over all the things as fast as you can right round the garden. And you mustn't miss anything out."

I began to laugh.

"Some things are quite wobbly," Molly called, holding out her arms to help me into the washing basket beside her. "And it was so funny when

Nelson hid in the chimney pot." She grinned and grabbed me in a hug. "We can race properly, Jack, now Ella's here."

Chapter 28
A New Ella

Dear Dad,

I took this photo especially for you.

The tall girl you can see laughing, with the long dark curly hair, is my friend Molly. And you know both the others. I like the way Mum is tickling Jack – he's doing his extreme giggling face. I like the way the sun makes Nelson's fur gleam and all the crazy furniture and things standing in the long grass.

I wanted to make Molly's house be all tidy and sorted out and it is, a bit. But best of all were the games we made up in the garden because Mum was joining in and Molly and Jack and me were running and chasing and all the extra furniture and chimney pots and boxes and stools made the best obstacle course ever.

Even though there's still lots to do, I realised we were going to be all right. You can't always sort out everything, but that's OK. You can still be happy even if there is some mess.

Do you know what I mean?

I wish you had been with us, Dad. I know you would have loved the obstacle course. But I know we can make another one when you come home.

Mum says hello again.

Ella

On Monday, in school, I felt a nudge beside me. "We've moved," chorused two voices. It was Rachel and Immy.

"We've come to sit next to you," Rachel said, flopping down and dumping her bag on the table.

"We've done a swap with Joshua and Marcus. Mr Hales said it's OK," Immy said.

I smiled. "That's brilliant."

Over at the other side of the room, Lydia was standing behind her table, still in her coat, gripping her school bag, staring at me with furious piercing eyes. "Sophie's away," Immy said, following my stare. "And Zing has asked to move to the front to sit with Emily."

I went on staring at Lydia.

"How's your mum, Molly?" I heard Immy ask.

"She's getting better," I heard Molly say, "much better."

Lydia slowly took out her pencil case, looked down at the wide grey tabletop and smoothed it with her hand. Her mouth twitched.

I turned and smiled at Immy.

"This is a great place to sit," Immy said. "You can see the playground from here. And Mr Hales says we have to plan our Christmas assembly in groups. We'll all be able to work together."

"I can't believe it's almost Christmas," I said.

"Too noisy, that group by the window," Mr Hales called, looking over at us. "You're all supposed to be reading."

"I am reading," Immy murmured.

We all giggled and pulled our reading books from our bags.

✗

In the last art club before the Christmas holidays I had Molly beside me.

Miss Denby brought lemonade and cakes for us all and we all made cards with Christmas trees.

As we were all packing up, Miss Denby came over.

"Molly's spending part of Christmas with us," I told her.

She winked at me and said, "I want to see lots more of your photos after the Christmas break. And lots more fantastic sketches from you, Molly."

Molly smiled and went on tidying away the paints.

"I'm thinking we might have an exhibition after Christmas, if you are all keen," Miss Denby told everyone. "Lydia, will you be coming along again next term?"

"I might do drama," came Lydia's sharp reply from the other side of the room. "See if that's more interesting."

Miss Denby caught my eye and did a tiny eye-roll. "Good idea. Ella here would never have realised her special talent for photography if she hadn't tried out lots of different things, would you, Ella?"

Snap! Lydia slammed her art case shut. "I can't stay chatting. I'm going to Hannah's cinema party." She pushed past me and made for the door. "I must go home and get ready."

I caught the sneer at the side of her mouth as she stared at Molly and me.

"We'd better get going, Molly," I called, grabbing my bag. "Hannah invited us too. Hope you have a nice Christmas, Miss Denby!"

Dear Dad,

Mum says we can come on an actual visit to you at Christmas when we are staying at Grandma's. Hooray!

Mum says see you soon.

I'm so happy we're coming to see you. I

am going to bring you some banana and chocolate chip cake. I'm practising making it. Here is a photo of some.
Love, Ella

I'm still a pair person really, I think.

I'm always going to be somewhere round the edge in school. But now I've found Molly she seems to understand what I'm thinking. She's like me.

I've realised I quite like being on the outside; I can watch everything that's going on.

Dear Ella,
I'm so happy you are coming, love. Say thank you to Mum. See you at Christmas.
Love you.
Dad